P
Val

Valentine's Night was recognized by national
bookstore chains across North America as the
bestselling Harlequin Presents for the year.
Penny Jordan's work is a favorite of romance readers
the world over; over fifty million copies of her books
have sold internationally in more than twenty languages.

"The game's over, Cousin Val," Sorrel told him firmly.

"If you say so," he agreed obligingly.

"So you admit that it *was* a game," Sorrel said, pouncing, "and that I *didn't*, that I didn't beg…ask you to take my clothes off?" Her face was red by the time she finished, but she was determined to stand her ground.

"Can't you remember?" Val asked her softly.

Damn him, he had caught her out again, and the infuriating thing was that she *couldn't* remember—not a damn thing apart from a delicious feeling of warmth and blissful security.

"I may be a raw colonial, but in my part of the world we never discuss what a lady—er—may or may not have said in an intimate situation."

PENNY JORDAN

VALENTINE'S NIGHT

Harlequin Books

TORONTO • NEW YORK • LONDON
AMSTERDAM • PARIS • SYDNEY • HAMBURG
STOCKHOLM • ATHENS • TOKYO • MILAN
MADRID • WARSAW • BUDAPEST • AUCKLAND

ISBN 0-373-60074-7

VALENTINE'S NIGHT

Dear Reader,

Step into the Winner's Circle, with a set of special romance novels guaranteed to win your heart!

In this outstanding selection of Harlequin and Silhouette books, we've chosen to showcase award winners, those novels that professional lovers of romance are always talking about, and readers can never forget. Some of your favorite authors have contributed their works to this collection, including Anne Stuart, Penny Jordan, Curtiss Ann Matlock, Dallas Schulze, Kathleen Korbel and Glenda Sanders.

Look for the Winner's Circle insignia on a new title each month from January to June, and you'll know you've picked a winner!

Happy reading...

The Editors of Harlequin and Silhouette books

CHAPTER ONE

'WHAT on earth are we going to do? We simply can't ask her *not* to come—not when she's been to such trouble to find us. She'd be hurt. But she *can't* stay here...not at the moment. The house is full to bursting point as it is.'

Sympathetically Sorrel watched the anxiety darken her mother's eyes. It was true that the unscheduled visit could not have come at a worse time. With the twins home from university, and her newly married elder brother and his wife taking up temporary accommodation with her parents, *and* Uncle Giles more or less a permanent house guest, the farm was already bursting at the seams.

Add to that the fact that her father's prize ewes were lambing ahead of time and he was consequently a little short-tempered with concern, and it was obvious that now was not precisely an ideal time for the family to receive into its bosom an unknown second cousin, heaven only knew how many times removed, from Australia. A cousin, moreover, whom none of them knew anything about, other than that her typed letter was written with such a breezy, not to say slightly overpowering, *bonhomie,* that made it very difficult for her mother to write back, and say no, they could not accommodate her as a guest.

'Normally I'd have loved to have her staying here,' her mother continued unhappily. 'But...'

'Why don't you write and explain the situation?' Sorrel suggested practically. They were sitting in the farmhouse kitchen, their conversation interrupted by the increasingly noisy protests of the orphaned lambs her mother was hand-rearing. 'Suggest that she delays her visit until later in the year.'

'I can't,' came the worried response. 'The letter went to the old farm, instead of coming here. Val obviously doesn't realise that we've moved and that the old farmhouse has been empty since Uncle Giles moved out. The letter would be lying up there yet if Simon hadn't driven over to show Fiona the house.'

'Oh, he's shown it to her, then,' Sorrel asked interestedly. 'What did she think? It's very remote, I know, and not exactly equipped with all mod cons...'

'Oh, she came back bubbling over with enthusiasm, and I can understand why. It's very hard to start off your married life living with your in-laws.'

'Mum, you've bent over backwards to make her feel at home,' Sorrel protested loyally.

'Oh, she isn't complaining—far from it, but I remember how I felt when I had to move in with Gran and Gramps. Of course, it was different for me. Unlike Fiona, I didn't come from farming stock. She's adapted marvellously well. She goes out in all weathers helping Simon and your dad with the stock, and she didn't seem a bit put off by the old farm's remoteness. I warned her that there are times when the snow closes off the road, and of course there's no gas or electricity up there at the moment, but your dad was saying it would be worth while having them installed, because if Simon and Fiona did move up there it would mean they could make far more use of the high pastures than he's been able to do.'

Sorrel was familiar enough with the complex family relationship which had led to her father inheriting not just his parents' farm, but his maternal uncle's as well. Since this latter farm was situated in the richer pastures of Shropshire, as opposed to his parents' farm in the Welsh mountains, he had moved his family down into Shropshire when Sorrel was a little girl, leaving his uncle Giles to take over the running of the Welsh land. Two years ago, following a bad bout of pneumonia, Giles had finally admitted that the rugged life of a hill farmer was getting too much for him, and since then the farmhouse had remained untenanted other than during the summer months when

Simon lived up there, watching over their sheep flocks.

They were an odd mixture, her parents: her father came from a long, long line of men who had been Welsh farmers; her mother had been a city girl who had fallen madly and illogically in love with the young countryman while he was visiting the Royal Show at Smithfield one year looking for a new pedigree ram; and their four children mirrored the quixotic blend of their parents. Simon, the eldest, whose feel for the land he had inherited fully from his father and who had never wanted to do anything other than follow in his footsteps. The twins: James the would-be scientist, who had always been irked by the constraining enclosure of the life his father and elder brother lived, who made no bones about his own desire to travel, to experience a wider knowledge of the world. Mark, the younger twin's expertise with anything mechanical had led to him training for a career in the computer industry, and yet he had retained that same deep love of the land that was so strong in their father and Simon.

And as for herself—well, she loved the land as well, but her mother claimed that the artistic talent which had led to her starting her own small, successful business designing and selling exclusive knitwear came from *her* side of the family. Like the colouring which had given Sorrel her name—her mane of russet hair was considered a little flamboyant by her father's family, as was her height and elegance of limb. Sorrel was not a Welsh Llewellyn, and yet—and yet she had a deep awareness of the richness of her heritage, of how lucky she had been born the child of two people each in their own way dedicated to bringing up their family in the kind of emotionally secure background that few of her peers had been privileged to experience.

Did the strength of her parents' marriage mean that she was more or less well-equipped to deal with the problems that seemed to destroy modern relationships? she wondered—more so since she had become engaged to Andrew.

Andrew did not come from farming stock. His father had been a solicitor in Ludlow. He was now dead, and Andrew's mother lived alone in their old family home. Andrew had an increasingly successful business in Ludlow buying and selling old books.

They had known one another since their schooldays, and if their relationship lacked a certain sparkle—a certain intensity—Sorrel knew she didn't mind, and that it wasn't possible to have everything in life. And besides, she had her own reasons for welcoming Andrew's calm courtship.

She knew that her family weren't entirely happy about her engagement to Andrew, but she was twenty-four, after all, and old enough to make up her own mind. If he sometimes niggled her with his pedantic, slightly old-fashioned ways—well, she reminded herself that *she* was far from perfect. But increasingly recently she had known that there was something vital lacking in their relationship... that their engagement was meandering towards no very certain conclusion, that Andrew's reserve and surely too old-fashioned decision that they should not be lovers until they were married was not romantic as she had first assumed, but indicative of some very problematic areas within their relationship. As was her own reluctance to pressure him into making love to her.

Surely she ought to feel differently? Surely she ought to want him more on a physical level? Was there something wrong with her that made her different from other young women her age? Did she have a much lower sexual drive than her peers?

She didn't have enough close female friends to know the answer. Those she had made at art college did not live locally, and the girls she had been at school with were now in the main married with families.

She knew the cause of her present dissatisfaction lay with her brother and his wife. No one seeing them together could doubt how they felt. Those looks they exchanged, those sneaked little touches... that flush that sometimes darkened Fiona's skin when she looked at Simon. No one could observe them together and not know how they felt. It was not like that with her and Andrew.

She really ought not to be sitting here in the kitchen with her mother, but working in the outbuilding her father had converted for her when she'd first set up in business on her own. However, her mother was still frowning over the problem of this unknown Australian female, who had written to them announcing that she had traced a relationship with their family and that, since she had business in the UK, she was coming over early so that she could spend a few days getting to know her relatives.

'So what are you going to do about her visit?' Sorrel asked her mother, who was expertly finishing feeding one lamb and starting on another.

'Well, it's too late to put her off. She's arriving the day after tomorrow. She says in her letter that she's hiring a car and that she'll drive straight here. Well, not here, of course, but to the old farmhouse.'

'We'll have to arrange to leave a message for her at the airport... explaining the position,' Sorrel suggested practically, but for some reason her mother didn't seem to find her suggestion acceptable.

'Oh, we can't do that!' she exclaimed. 'It would be so—so inhospitable. Think, darling, how you'd feel if you'd travelled all that way—'

'Uninvited,' Sorrel interrupted her drily, but her mother made no comment, saying instead,

'And we can't let her just arrive at the farm, driving all that way to find the place completely deserted. As you know, it's barely even furnished. Just that one bedroom that Simon uses, and the kitchen. I wish there was some way we could put her up here, but it's impossible—what with the twins at home and Uncle Giles and now Simon and Fiona, and it isn't even as though we could get a spare bed in your room, and I won't have the poor thing sleeping on a settee. What would she think of us? Of course, your uncle Giles is going to visit cousin Martha in Cardiff next week, and the twins are due back at university in three days, so it won't be for very long.'

'*What* won't?' Sorrel asked suspiciously, suddenly alerted to potential danger by the way her mother was deliberately avoiding looking at her.

'Well, your father and I talked it over, and there's really no reason why the two of you... Valerie and you... shouldn't stay up at the hill farm for a few days. Simon could drive up there with plenty of supplies. The house is dry enough. The Aga still works, and there are the oil lamps.'

'Mother, it's *impossible!* There's only one bed up there...'

'Yes, but it's a *double* bed, not like that tiny thing in your room. And besides, Valerie specifically said how much she was looking forward to seeing the farm. Did you know that her ancestor was born there? Imagine that—and then to travel all the way out to Australia.'

'Mm. Willingly? Or was he one of the family's black sheep?' Sorrel asked wryly. 'Mother, *think,* what if we don't get on? We'll be stuck up there for three whole days.'

'Well, you could always come here for your meals.'

'Mum, it's a one-and-a-half-hour drive,' Sorrel pointed out firmly. 'I understand how you feel, but surely we could arrange for her to stay at one of the hotels in Ludlow for a few days?'

'Impossible. I've already tried that. They're booked up already with people getting ready for the festival.'

'But that's months away,' Sorrel protested, and then, as she saw the tiredness and anxiety in her mother's eyes, she suddenly relented. 'Well, I suppose there's no reason why I shouldn't spend a few days up there.'

'You used to love staying up there with Gran and Gramps,' her mother reminded her eagerly.

'Yes, during the summer, not in the middle of March, and in those days I think the main attraction was that I was madly in love with the history of the place, and spent most of my time daydreaming of border skirmishes and valiant Welshmen pitting their meagre forces against the might of their English overlords.'

'And that's another thing,' her mother said brightly. 'Your cousin says in her letter how much she's looking forward to learning more about the area. She'll love hearing all about its history, and you've always taken far more of an interest in that than the others. Not that I could send one of the twins up there to stay with her...'

'Why not?' Sorrel questioned mock-innocently. 'She's as much their cousin as she is mine.'

'Sorrel, you know exactly what I mean. She's a girl. It wouldn't... it wouldn't be proper. Not with only that one double bed up there,' she said severely, breaking off as she heard Sorrel laughing. 'Oh, you knew exactly what I meant all along! I...'

She stopped talking as her eldest son walked into the kitchen; Simon paused to remove his filthy wellington boots before turning round and saying to Fiona, who was standing behind him, 'Give me the lambs and I'll take them over to the Aga.'

'Oh, not more,' Sorrel complained, her heart stirred to pity, nevertheless, by the sight of the two tiny, immobile creatures.

'Twins,' Simon told her grimly. 'We've lost the ewe, and by the looks of it we might lose these two as well. Dad's going berserk. None of them should have lambed so early, and he can't get hold of the vet.'

Expertly ministering to the two small creatures, Sorrel was relieved to see that they were still alive. Fiona came into the kitchen on the heels of her husband.

'Simon, you're going to have to drive up to the old farm when you can. Sorrel's agreed to stay there a few days with Valerie, just until the boys are back at university and we can find room for her down here.'

'Ma conned you into it, then, did she?' Simon muttered *sotto voce* to his sister, and then, turning to his wife, said calmly, 'Come on, cough up, that's fifty pence you owe me.'

'What? Oh, I might have known!' Sorrel grimaced. Her mother was a great strategist, a compulsive plotter and planner.

'Now, Simon, that's enough,' she told her eldest son firmly, but when he winked at Sorrel behind his mother's bent back Sorrel had no doubts at all that she had well and truly been caught. And it was too late to back out now. Too late to protest as she ought to have done, that she was far too busy to spend three days with a completely unknown female with whom she most probably had nothing whatsoever in common, apart from their family name.

'IT WON'T BE SO bad,' her mother consoled her over supper later on that day. 'You'll be able to show her the diaries. I'm sure she'll love those.'

'Are they still up there?' Sorrel asked her.

'Mmm . . . packed away in the attic. I'll ask Simon to bring them down for you when he goes up there.'

'It's a lovely old house,' Fiona chipped in.

'But very remote,' Sorrel reminded her, adding with a grin, 'but *you* won't mind that, will you?'

And the whole family laughed at the look Simon and his new wife exchanged, although it was Simon's turn to laugh when he told them smugly, 'We may not be on our own for very long.'

'Oh, Simon, it's too soon yet to be sure,' Fiona protested. Watching them, Sorrel felt an unfamiliar and unwanted sensation of envy clamp her heart.

What would it be like to love someone the way Fiona loved Simon? To want nothing other than to be a part of his life, to conceive his children . . .

Her relationship with Andrew wasn't like that. She loved him, of course she did. He would make her an excellent husband, but when she didn't see him for a few days, for instance, she had no yearning to do so. No sense of loss when he went away to one of his frequent conferences or sales. He was away at the moment; she hadn't seen him for over a week, and yet she was quite content. She didn't go to bed at night hungering for his unexciting kisses, wishing time would speed past so that they could be married, so that she could lie in his arms at night as Fiona undoubtedly lay in Simon's. She felt none of the things so very evident in her sister-in-law's rosy face, and until recently it hadn't bothered her; but now for some reason it did, and illogically she decided that the root cause of all this dissatisfaction was the unplanned and unwanted visit of this Australian relative who was thrusting herself into their lives, claiming a kinship with them which might or might not exist. And now she had agreed to spend three days with her. How on earth was she going to keep her entertained?

Plas Gwynd was ten miles from the nearest farm and over fifteen from the nearest village. It clung to the hillside, gaunt and grey, weathered by over five hundred years of storms, a long, rambling collection of outbuildings and farmhouse which had housed her family for generation upon generation.

In the spring and summer, the garden bloomed so profusely that it took one's breath away, and it was true that the lee of the hill gave the house some degree of protection, but there was nothing to protect the sheep from the winter snows, no one with whom to share the weather's fierceness, and it was no wonder that her father had preferred to farm the much richer Shropshire pastures left to him by his maternal uncle rather than remain living in the remote Welsh farmhouse.

Hill farming was backbreaking, grinding work. No hill farmer was ever rich, and her father was fortunate in his fertile English pastures.

After supper, Sorrel went out to the barn which housed her knitting machine and design studio. She often worked best late at night when her thoughts became miraculously clear and concise, free of the clutter of the day.

Some of her inspiration came from what she saw around her, or what she had experienced as a child. Once she had realised how fascinating she found the design and execution of knitwear, she had spent several holidays in Scotland, studying the traditional knitting patterns and stitches they had used there for generations. Some of her designs, though, were very modern, incorporating innovative ideas and vibrant modern colours.

In her bedroom, thrown across her bed, was the woollen rug which she had designed herself at art school, and which she had kept for sentiment's sake. She still designed such rugs and they sold well . . . as did the tapestry cushions she had started as a sideline two years ago and which were increasingly in demand.

Her glance fell on a tapestry frame holding the beginnings of a new design she was trying out. She could take that to the farm with her. It would give her something to do if her cousin's company became too much.

The hill farm wasn't even equipped with a telephone. There was no gas, no electricity, although apparently her father planned to have these services installed for Simon and Fiona. Sighing faintly, Sorrel switched off the lights and headed back to the house.

'YOU'VE GOT everything, then? Blankets, sheets, towels, soap, the boxes of food? Simon says there's paraffin and oil up there for the lamps, and he's putting some bags of logs and fuel in the back of the Land Rover for the Aga.'

'Ma, we'll be there for three days, not three months,' Sorrel reminded her mother patiently.

'Yes, I know, but Giles said this morning that he fancied there was bad weather on the way.'

'Well, if there is, there wasn't anything about it on the farming forecast,' Simon told his mother cheerfully.

'Maybe not, but your uncle lived in the mountains for most of his life.'

'He's an old man, Ma,' Simon said gently. 'Sometimes he gets confused. Don't start looking for problems. Ready, Sorrel?' he asked his sister.

'Just about,' Sorrel agreed. She wasn't looking forward to the next three days one little bit, but her mother was so relieved, so pleased, that she hadn't the heart to back out. After all, they would proba-

bly pass quickly enough, and she had to admit that
her mother did have a point. It did seem a little inhospitable after this Valerie had come such a long
way to tell her that they didn't have room for her.
And who could tell... it might be rather nice having another female in the family; her bad mood of
the previous evening was lightening. How old was
she? Sorrel wondered, as Simon finished loading
the Land Rover, and climbed into the driver's seat.

'Let's hope she's going to be able to find the
place,' she commented to her brother an hour and
a half later as they turned off the country road and
into the muddy, rutted lane that led to the farm.

'Well, it's well signposted enough, although she
only needs to miss the turning in the village... What
time is she due?'

'I don't know. Mum said her flight got into
Heathrow at midday, so I expect it will be some
time later this afternoon. Will you stay and meet
her?'

'Can't,' Simon told her, shaking his head. 'Half
a dozen more ewes are showing signs of starting
with their lambs.'

He pulled up abruptly in the cobbled yard and
opened the door. Sorrel shivered as she felt the drop
in temperature. It was far colder here than it had
been at home; the winter landscape bare of trees,
rawly bleak. The mountains in the distance were

snow-covered, as was the peak of the one behind the house, the ground underfoot frozen.

'Let's get this stuff inside,' Simon announced, heaving down the sacks of fuel and carrying it into the lean-to porch that sheltered the back door.

The door opened straight into the stone-flagged kitchen, the stone floor striking chill through the thin soles of Sorrel's boots and making her shiver.

'It's summer now in Australia, isn't it?' she asked through chattering teeth. 'I wonder if this Val realises how cold it is here.'

'It just feels it because the house has been empty. Wait until we've got the range lit.'

'I'll do that,' Sorrel told him, knowing he was anxious to start back. 'You bring the rest of the stuff in.'

She filled a small kettle and had just set it to boil on the emergency gas ring she had brought with her when Simon came in with the last load. The range was now lit and the chill just beginning to ease off the kitchen.

'I'll fill the lamps with oil,' Simon told her. 'I checked upstairs when I came with Fiona. The bedroom isn't damp, so you should be OK. Remember to keep the range in, though, otherwise you'll have no hot water.'

'Don't even mention it,' Sorrel groaned.

'Why don't you light a fire upstairs?'

Sorrel had forgotten that the main bedroom had a working fireplace. In view of the unexpected iciness of the wind and the frozen ground outside, it seemed a good idea.

She made Simon a cup of tea while he checked that there was nothing left in the Land Rover and that she would be comfortable and safe.

Once he had gone, Sorrel didn't feel alone, as she had expected. Perhaps because there was so much still to do.

The bedroom, as he had said, was dry but very cold. She lit the fire, and once she had assured herself that it was going properly, mentally thanking heaven for the convenience of modern firelighters, she set about making up the old-fashioned double bed with its wooden footboard and headboard. It had to be polished first, and the faint smell of beeswax that hovered in the air after she had finished this task reminded her very much of her childhood visits to her grandparents.

Her mother had wisely sent up a very large duckdown duvet and, a little to Sorrel's surprise, the patchwork cover which had originally covered the bed and which had been made by her grandmother as part of her trousseau.

Once that was on the bed, the fire casting dancing shadows on the plain white walls, the room suddenly took on a cosy, homely look. Unlike the old-fashioned bathroom, which felt as though it was refrigerated, Sorrel reflected, her teeth starting to chatter before she had been in it for more than five minutes.

It needed, as her mother had forecast, cleaning, and by the time she had performed this chore she was beginning to feel a bit warmer. Even so, she did not envy her grandparents having to leave the warmth of their bedroom on a cold winter morning to come in here.

Downstairs the range was now thoroughly warming the kitchen, and Sorrel polished the large oak dresser which was set into one wall, unpacking the crockery from home and putting it on the shelves. It looked rather lost on a dresser designed to show off an entire family dinner service.

At first she was so busy that the sudden change in the quality of the light from outside didn't strike her, and then a certain betraying silence, a certain inborn instinct, made her lift her head and go to the window. Her heart sank as she saw the snow swirling down outside.

Uncle Giles had been right, after all. She only hoped that it wasn't snowing in Ludlow. If it was, her mother would be having forty fits of anxiety.

What time was it? She looked at her watch. Just gone four. Too early yet for the appearance of Valerie, if indeed she *could* still appear. If the weather deteriorated as dramatically as it could do at this height, the hill pass would soon be blocked and the farm would be cut off. It happened almost every winter.

Everything was ready now and there was nothing she could do other than wait...and hope that Cousin Val did not get stuck somewhere in the snow.

She lived in Perth, the beautiful town on the Swan River where Sorrel, whose knowledge of Australia's weather was only sketchy, suspected they did not have the winters suffered by the Welsh hills. She wondered how Val's parents felt about their daughter going half-way across the world to visit unknown relatives. What would she be like?

Sorrel filled the kettle and placed it on the hob of the old-fashioned range and then went to the window.

Already the landscape had turned white, the low stone walls thickly covered in snow. The wind had increased, driving the flakes into a frenzy of blizzarding white violence that eddied and whirled in front of the farm, changing the landscape as she watched.

Sorrel shivered. She was safe enough here inside the old farmhouse, and Simon would be back in three days, but she would hate to be driving in this weather. How far had her cousin got? To Ludlow perhaps, with its historic castle, now merely a ruin, but even in its destruction impressive, giving to the imaginative a strong sense of what its power must

once have been. The redstone fortress on the River
Teme conjured up to Sorrel's eyes vivid impres-
sions of all that it had once been.

Or had Val already driven through Ludlow and
into the Welsh hills?

The kettle sang and Sorrel shivered. She felt
restless and ill at ease in a way that was unfamiliar
to her, alien to her normal placidity and calmness.
Her placid nature was one of the things Andrew
admired most about her. For some reason or other,
that seemed to amuse her family. It was true that as
a child she had often been driven to quick-tempered
outbursts against her brothers, but she had outgrown such childishness long ago. She sat down in
front of her tapestry, trying to concentrate on the
stitches. It was an ambitious project, unlike any of
her previous work—something she was doing
purely for the creative pleasure it gave her; something along the lines of a medieval wall-covering,
depicting the four seasons in relation to the traditional work of the farmer's wife. She was doing it
as a special gift for her mother, who had often remarked that the bare galleried landing of the old
farmhouse cried out for some kind of tapestry.

The Shropshire farmhouse was even older than
the Welsh one, but its Tudor-style beams and wat-
tle and daub walls gave it a soft prettiness that the
more sturdy stone Welsh building lacked.

The light was fading rapidly, and Sorrel had to get up to light the lamps and to go upstairs and check on the fire. The bedroom felt deliciously warm now, although the bathroom was still icy cold. She hadn't investigated the other bedrooms, which she knew would be bare of their furniture and very cold.

Simon had brought down a box from the attic which contained the old diaries, and on impulse Sorrel kneeled down on the floor beside it and lifted one out.

It had been a tradition that the women of the Llewellyn family kept diaries, originally merely to record the events of their working year: to record details of their produce from the kitchen gardens, to list the ingredients of herbal remedies and the money paid out for those household necessities which could not be made at home.

Their farm had been a productive one compared with many, but even so it made Sorrel wince to realise how hard their lives must have been.

She was so deeply engrossed that it was gone six o'clock before she lifted her head from the book. She went to the window and could see nothing in the dark, so, picking up one of the lanterns, she opened the door.

The moment she opened the outer porch door, the wind blew in fierce eddies of snow, the lamp flickering wildly as she held it up.

Beyond the farmyard lay a sea of white. Deep drifts blocked the drive. No car could possibly get through them, and even a Land Rover would have had problems. There was no way Cousin Val was going to be able to make it to the farmhouse now and, mingled with Sorrel's feeling of relief that she had been spared the three days' intimate company of a woman she had no idea how she was going to get on with, she had a prickling sensation of apprehension as she wondered where on earth her cousin was.

And it wasn't even as though the farm had a telephone and she could alert her family to the situation.

If anything, the temperature had dropped even lower, and just those few minutes' exposure to the cold had turned her fingers numb and was making her shiver. Sorrel was glad to get back inside.

The remoteness of the farm caused her no fear, and neither did she find the thought of her own company disturbing. It struck her that by rights she ought to be yearning for Andrew to be with her, but when she thought of her fiancé it was in the knowledge that, if he were here, he would be alternately complaining and worrying.

Andrew was devoted to his business, fussy to the point of irritation about his appearance and that of the small flat above the bookshop. He would hate the farmhouse with its lack of amenities.

When they got married they planned to find a house in Ludlow, and she would then use Andrew's present flat as her workshop; at least, that was what she had suggested, and Andrew had seemed to go along with her idea. It was odd, when she thought about it, how they had got engaged. They had been dating casually for a few months, and then Andrew had taken her to see his great-aunt, and it had been while they were there that the subject of an engagement had first come up.

The old lady had been extremely forthright in her views and speech, and she had commented that it was high time Andrew settled down and produced his family; he was too old to remain single any longer without becoming eccentric.

And then it had been on the way home that he had proposed to her...stumbling over the words a little, making her aware of both how much she liked him and how vulnerable he was. He had wanted to buy her a ring, but in the end they had decided to save the money instead. At twenty-four, she felt she was too mature to need the visible trappings of their commitment to one another. Only, recently that commitment hadn't seemed quite so strong, on either of their parts.

The sudden sound of someone banging on the outer door made her jump. She got up uncertainly and hurried towards the kitchen door, opening it and stepping into the porch.

As she reached for the outer door, the knock sounded again, demanding impatiently that she hurry.

She fumbled with the lock and then turned the handle. The wind caught the door, pushing it back so hard it almost knocked her over, and a very Australian and irritable male voice proclaimed 'At last! Thank heaven for that.'

Cousin Val... it had to be. But by no strength of the imagination was Cousin Val what she had expected... what any of them had expected.

'This *is* the Llewellyn farm, isn't it?' the Australian voice demanded, and Sorrel nodded. Her own voice seemed to have deserted her for some reason. Temporary paralysis caused by shock, she told herself, as she stepped back into the kitchen. The shock of discovering that Cousin Val was not, as they had all supposed, a woman, but a man... Very much a man, Sorrel acknowledged as he followed her inside the kitchen, shrugging off a snow-covered sheepskin jacket as he did so, and then bending to tug off his wellingtons.

'I thought I wasn't going to make it,' he told her calmly. 'I had to abandon my car way down the bottom of the lane. Fact is, I had no idea there was going to be this kind of weather.' He looked round the kitchen and frowned, picking up her tension.

'Is something wrong? You did get my letter?'

'Oh, yes, we got your letter,' Sorrel told him bitterly. 'But we assumed, because you signed it Val, that the Val was short for Valerie.'

'Valerie?' He stared at her. The snow had melted on his head, revealing thick black hair, well-cut and clinging damply now to his skull.

As he stood up, she realised how tall he was, how very broad-shouldered, even without the enveloping sheepskin.

'We thought you were a girl,' Sorrel told him tensely.

He gave her a slow look. His eyes, she realised, were grey—cool and hard as granite.

'Did you, now?' He seemed faintly amused. 'I suppose I should have thought of that. The Val is short for Valentine... a family name on my mother's side. She was part Russian. So you thought I was a girl. Well, as you can see, I'm not. It doesn't matter, does it?'

Doesn't matter? she thought! Just wait until he knew!

'As a matter of fact, it does,' she said as calmly as she could. 'You see, this farmhouse is no longer occupied and we didn't realise you were planning to visit us until it was too late to let you know what a bad time you'd picked—'

'What do you mean, it isn't occupied? *You're* living here, aren't you?'

He seemed more annoyed than concerned, and for some reason that annoyed her.

He had walked past her without so much as a 'by your leave', and was standing in front of the range. The small canvas bag he had brought in with him was still on the floor, snow melting on it.

'I left the rest of my stuff in the car. How long is this snow likely to last?'

'I don't know!' Sorrel told him grittily. She had seldom experienced the antagonism towards anyone that she was experiencing now, and never without undue provocation. So what was it about this man, with his air of easy self-assurance, that so rubbed her up the wrong way? She could feel herself bristling like a defensive cat confronted by a large dog. She didn't want him invading her space. She didn't want him *anywhere* near her, she realised.

'Mm... Well, someone must know. Where's the rest of the family?'

'Not here,' Sorrel told him succinctly, and had the pleasure of seeing him momentarily disconcerted.

CHAPTER TWO

APART from the hissing of the kettle which Sorrel had filled automatically and set on the hob, the kitchen was silent with tension. Then Val broke the tension, saying curtly, 'Let me get this straight. Your parents don't have the room to put me up right now, so, thinking that I was a young woman, they press-ganged you into coming up here to welcome me and stay with me until such time as your twin brothers go back to university.'

'*I* didn't say I was press-ganged,' Sorrel said stiffly.

'You didn't have to,' came the dry response. 'It was written all over you.'

'Oh, I see. You only need to take one look at a person and you know immediately what they're thinking, is that it?' she snapped at him, and then was appalled with herself. How on earth had she allowed him to get so dangerously under her skin that he could provoke her this easily?

Dangerously under her skin? A tingle of apprehension shivered over her body.

'It seemed the most sensible solution. If we'd had the slightest idea that you—'

'Yeah, I know. Nothing would have persuaded you to come up here if you'd known you were going to have to spend three days alone with a man. Hell, I thought modern women were supposed to be fully emancipated. Let me tell you, lady, in Australia it's the male of the species who needs to protect himself from the female, not the other way around, especially if he's made himself a bit of money.'

'Really?' Sorrel looked down her nose at him. 'Am I to presume that you're speaking from personal experience or merely hearsay?'

There was a moment's silence, during which he gave her a lightning look of such chilling intensity that she almost shivered. She had struck a nerve there, no doubt about it, and privately she was astounded by her own recklessness. It was completely out of character for her to behave like this.

'Well, now,' he told her in a calm drawl, 'to use an American phrase, that's for me to know and you—'

'And you can keep the knowledge to yourself,' Sorrel interrupted him, hot flags of temper burning in her cheeks. She wasn't used to men who treated her like this: men who dominated their surroundings by their height and breadth, men who

practically oozed sexuality in a way that was posi-
tively unnerving.

The kettle reached the boil and started to sing.
Sorrel reached for it automatically, and then cried
out as she forgot about the metal handle and
scorched her skin.

Instantly Valentine was at her side, moving with
surprising speed for such a large man, whipping up
a cloth and removing the kettle from her burned
hand, rushing her over to the sink to swish icy-cold
water over her hot, blistered skin.

She tried to pull away, to regain control of the
situation, but his body trapped her against the sink.
She was a tall girl—taller, in fact, than Andrew and
her father, but Valentine was at least a head taller.
He made her feel fragile and vulnerable in a way
that made her heart thump—or was that just the
effect of the adrenalin released by her pain?

'Have you anything to put on this?' he asked her
tersely.

Sorrel nodded. 'There's a medicine chest upstairs in the bathroom. I'll get it. It will be quicker,'
she added, when she saw he was going to object.
'It's only a small burn.'

Once upstairs, she refrained from giving in to the
cowardly impulse to shut herself in the bedroom
and stay there. Her mother had never dreamed of
this outcome when she had cosily announced that

Sorrel and her cousin could share the large double bed.

Valentine would simply have to sleep downstairs. But on what? There were only a couple of easy chairs in the kitchen, and no spare bedding at all.

When she got back downstairs, she found him pouring out two mugs of tea. He handed her one of the mugs, and although the tea was rather stronger than she liked she took it gratefully.

'So, how long are we likely to be cooped up here together?' he asked her once she had assured him that her hand, although painful, was not badly burned.

'Well, the twins go back to university at the end of the week, but I don't know how long the snow will last. Simon *should* be able to get through with the Land Rover.'

'But he won't arrive for another three days?'

Sorrel shook her head.

'Well, I guess unless the snow clears, we're stuck with one another.' He saw her face pale and raised his eyebrows.

'Burn bothering you?'

'No,' Sorrel told him shortly, in a voice that announced that she didn't like his questions.

'Well, something is,' he persisted, ignoring her coldness. 'Look, it's a long time since I last drove through snow, and since you've made it plain just how you feel about my company, if you could just show me where I'm supposed to sleep...' He saw her face and frowned.

'*Now* what's wrong?'

There was no way she could avoid it. She looked at him and said hollowly, 'There's only one bed-room—furnished, I mean. You see, when Uncle Giles left, Mum and Dad moved the furniture out, just leaving the one bed for Simon when he comes here during the summer.'

His eyes narrowed disconcertingly, suddenly boring into her with an intentness nothing in his previous demeanour had led her to expect. She had the odd notion that she was suddenly seeing the real man, and that the cloak of *bonhomie* and laid-back insouciance he had shown her before was just exactly that. It gave her an uncomfortable jolt to be subjected to that hard grey stare.

'What do you mean, one bed?'

'Exactly what I said,' Sorrel mumbled uncomfortably. 'The old bed that belonged to Gran and Gramps was so heavy that Mum and Dad left it. I brought clean bedding with me, of course, but only enough for that bed.'

There was a long pause, and then he said softly, 'I see... You mean that because your mother assumed that Val was short for Valerie and that I was therefore female, she saw no harm in the two of us sharing a bed.'

'She was panic-stricken,' Sorrel told him. 'She had no idea what to do. It was too late to get in touch with you to let you know the situation.'

'And that's why you've been behaving like a cat walking on hot desert sand, is it? The thought of having to sleep with me...'

'I am *not* going to sleep with you,' Sorrel told him indignantly, her face flaming. 'And yes, of course I was a little...embarrassed.'

'No need to be on my behalf,' he told her drily. 'You won't be the first woman I've shared a bed with.'

Sorrel stared at him, almost struck dumb with anger at his casual mockery of her. When she got her voice back, she said tightly, 'No, I'm sure I'm not. But unlike you, *I* haven't—' She broke off abruptly, but it was too late.

'You wouldn't by any chance be trying to tell me that you're still a virgin, would you?'

The way he said it made it sound as though she was some kind of freak, Sorrel thought wretchedly. Oh, what on earth had possessed her to be so stupid? Why hadn't she just kept quiet? She ached to be able to make some light-hearted comment that would cover her mistake and deceive him, but one look into those steel-grey eyes warned her that it was impossible. It was like looking into the heart of a steel trap.

'A virgin,' he mused, watching her. 'And you must be what . . . twenty-five—twenty-six?'

'Twenty-four, actually,' Sorrel snapped at him.

'You're not bad looking. Nice body . . . good legs,' he added appreciatively, skimming her body with thoughtful scrutiny. It's hard to guess what your breasts are like under that sweater, but my guess—'

He broke off as Sorrel gasped in indignation.

'Something wrong,' he asked her, lifting dark eyebrows.

'When I want your opinion on my body, I'll ask for it,' Sorrel told him grimly.

'No need to get so uptight. I was just curious to know why a woman like you hasn't had a lover. When I was your age . . .'

He was somewhere in his mid-thirties, Sorrel guessed, although, with the deep tanning of his skin and the tiny lines that fanned out from his eyes, it was hard to be accurate. There was certainly no grey in his hair. No discernible excess of flesh on his hard-muscled frame.

'I have no wish to know about your sexual experiences,' Sorrel told him frigidly.

'No man in your life, eh? Now . . .'

Sorrel had had enough. 'As a matter of fact, there *is* a man in my life. I'm engaged to be married, and if Andrew has too much respect for me to . . . to rush me into bed, then . . .'

She broke off as she heard his laughter. Hot spots of colour burned in her face as she glared at him.

'Too much respect? More like not enough guts,' Val told her forthrightly. 'What kind of man is he?'

'A decent, respectable, hardworking kind,' Sorrel told him grittily. 'Not that it's any business of yours.'

He was looking at her rather oddly, an almost devilish glint of amusement in his eyes.

'I see. And I suppose the sober, respectable...worthy fiancé would not approve of you spending the next three days and nights alone here with me?'

Sorrel opened her mouth to protest that Andrew would understand, and then she remembered how very narrow-minded he could be on occasions, how much importance he placed on respectability, and she swallowed back the words. He *would* understand, of course he would. And no one outside the family need know. The kind of speculation and gossip that Andrew would abhor wasn't going to arise because no one outside the family would ever know, would they?

She looked up and found that Val was watching her with cool amusement.

'Of course Andrew would understand,' she lied, tilting her chin and staring him down. 'He trusts me implicitly, and besides, there's no question of anything...well, illicit. It's just that there's been a mistake.'

'He trusts you, but he doesn't desire you. Sounds an odd basis for a lifetime commitment to me.'

'Just because sex isn't the most important part of our relationship, that's no reason to sneer at it,' Sorrel told him angrily.

'As far as I understand it, sex doesn't form *any* part of your relationship,' Val threw back at her. 'Lord, I thought your kind had gone out with the Victorians. What do the rest of the family think about this engagement?'

'They...they like Andrew,' Sorrel fibbed valiantly.

'You don't sound so certain. It seems to me that this engagement of yours has been a bad mistake.'

Sorrel couldn't believe her ears. She knew that Australians believed in frank speaking, but this was sheer rudeness. Thoroughly affronted, she opened her mouth to tell him that her private life was no concern of his when he forestalled her by changing the subject and saying, 'Any chance of anything to eat? We were late landing at Heathrow, and I never eat plane food.'

He made it sound as though he travelled a great deal, and Sorrel felt a faint unwanted stirring of curiosity about him.

His clothes, now that she looked at him properly, were expensive and well-tailored, despite their casual appearance. Looking at him, it would be impossible to judge just where he was from or what he did for a living.

'I've got a home-made shepherd's pie I could heat up. It will take about half an hour in the range.' She went to put it in. 'Your letter said that you had to come to England on business,' she went on abruptly. 'What kind of business?'

'I have a boat-building business in Perth, and I'm over here to check out a new British technique for making super-lightweight craft.'

'And you thought you'd look us up... just like that?'

Her aggression made him smile mockingly at her. Was there no way she could get under his skin the way he did hers? Sorrel thought crossly as she got the pie and put it in the oven, this time taking care to use protective oven gloves.

'Ancestry's very big back home at the moment. Something to do with the recent bicentennial fever, I guess. I knew that my family came originally from Wales, and I thought it might be interesting to have a go at seeing how far I could trace it back.'

'Llewellyn's a very common Welsh name,' Sorrel pointed out.

'I have a great-aunt who swears that she remembers hearing from her grandmother how her husband's father came originally from this part of

Wales. He was a Daniel, too, like your father. And the family diaries—'

'Your family keep diaries, too?' Sorrel's face lit up, her animosity forgotten. 'Oh, I'd love to see them. Ma asked Simon to bring ours down. She thought you might be interested in reading them. It's a tradition that the women of the family always keep a diary.' She stopped, annoyed with herself for forgetting how much she disliked him.

'What's this?' he asked her suddenly, staring at her tapestry frame.

She told him reluctantly, but her love and enthusiasm for her craft refused to give way to her desire to be abrupt with him.

'I've done the first three seasons,' she heard herself telling him, in a voice that was suddenly, for no reason at all, slightly breathy. It couldn't be because he had bent his head over her work, just in the direction she was pointing, so that his dark hair brushed against her wrist, causing tiny tingling sensations to race along her veins, heating her entire body, could it? No, of course not. It was unthinkable...ridiculous...impossible that she should react to this abrasive Australian in a way that she had never reacted to Andrew, the man she had agreed to marry.

Various alien and disturbing thoughts filled her mind, making the colour come up under her clear Celtic skin.

'And the final season?' Val prompted.

'Winter,' she told him curtly.

'Yes... The last time I experienced snow like this was in the Canadian Rockies during my university days. I hadn't realised you could have this kind of weather so late in the year.'

'Half a dozen or more climbers who think the same thing lose their lives in these mountains almost every year,' Sorrel told him. 'You were lucky not to be trapped inside your car. Why did you go to university in Canada?'

He raised his eyebrows a little but, if he could ask her impertinent questions about her relationship with Andrew, then she was quite sure that she could reciprocate. It was odd how curious she was about him. Dangerous, too. She shivered a little, a tiny frisson of unfamiliar apprehension-laced excitement going through her.

'I wanted to study geology, and I spent a post-graduate year in the Rockies doing fieldwork.'

'Geology? I thought you said you built boats.'

'I do—now. The pie smells as though it's ready.'

In other words, no more questions. He was adroit at concealing more of himself than he revealed, and even more adroit at getting her to reveal far too much, she acknowledged as she went over to the oven.

The pie *was* almost ready. There were fresh vegetables to go with it, and rhubarb fool for pudding.

'We ought to be toasting our new-found cousinship,' Val remarked as he asked Sorrel where he could find the cutlery. 'Is there anything to drink?'

Her mother had packed a couple of bottles of her home-made wine, and Sorrel produced one of them. She saw his eyebrows lift in a way that was becoming familiar as he studied the label, and she explained to him what elderberry wine was.

'A resourceful woman, your mother.'

'She's a home-maker,' Sorrel told him, 'and she thrives on hard work. She's spent her life doing all the things we're told turn the female sex into drudges, and yet I've never met a more fulfilled woman than my mother. She's interested in everything and everyone...and she knows so much about the history of the wife's role in the running of a farm like ours. She sometimes gives talks on it to local WI meetings. She loves it...standing up on the stage, talking to them...and they love her. I asked her a few years ago if she had ever thought what she might have done if she'd had a career. She laughed at me. She said that being married to my father gave her the best of everything: a man whom she loved, his children, the pleasure of running her own home, and the business aspects of keeping the farm accounts, of being free to order her own day, to enjoy the countryside. I know what she means...I don't think I could ever work for a large organisation with regimented rules and regulations after being my own boss.'

'I know what you mean,' Val told her, surprising her. 'When I started off in mineral exploration, it was very much a free and easy life. You got a job working for a newly formed company. They bought the mineral right to a certain tract of land and sent you out to discover what, if any, value it might have. You lived in the outback...often for weeks at a time, turning in a report when you'd finished the job. But once the boom came, the pleasure went out of it.'

'Was that why you build boats instead?'

'Sort of. This wine smells good... Not quite up to our better Australian vineyards' products, of course.'

'It's very potent,' Sorrel warned him, dishing up their meal and putting a plateful of food in front of him.

It had surprised her a little that he had so readily and naturally helped her with the preparation of the meal, but perhaps if he had lived alone in the outback he was used to fending for himself. She had always thought that Australian men were very chauvinistic, and considered women to be little more than chattels.

Fair-mindedly, she acknowledged that she did not really know enough about the continent or its inhabitants to separate truth from myth, and it was probable that Australian men, like any men, were a mixed and varied bunch of human beings who should not be typecast.

'This is good,' Val told her appreciatively, tucking into his food. 'Your mother's an excellent cook.'

Sorrel bent her head over her own plate, not telling him that *she* had made the pie. She enjoyed cooking, and firmly believed that any form of creative achievement could be satisfying when one was well-taught. Although her mother was what was normally referred to as a plain cook, she took a pride in the meals she placed before her family, and she had passed on that pride to Sorrel.

Val had poured them both a glass of wine, and now he put down his knife and fork and picked up his glass, motioning to Sorrel to do the same.

'To you, Sorrel Llewellyn,' he toasted her softly. 'I'm delighted to make your acquaintance... Drink it,' he urged her when she barely touched her lips to the glass. 'Otherwise I'm going to think it's poisoned. You certainly looked at me as though you'd have loved to slip me a glass of hemlock when I first arrived.'

'It was a shock to discover you were a man,' Sorrel protested, letting the warming wine slide down her throat. It tasted delicious but, as she well remembered from past occasions, she really did not have a strong enough head to cope with her mother's potent home-made brews.

Over their meal they talked, or rather Val talked and she listened, so that by the time they were ready for their pudding she was beginning to feel almost lazily content.

She started to get up to take their plates to the sink, but Val forestalled her, announcing that it was his turn to do some work.

As he walked past her chair he refilled her glass and she stared at it owlishly. Was that the third or fourth time he had filled it? She felt too pleasantly hazy to worry...too interested in the stories Val was telling her about his research into the family.

He had already explained to her that his name was Russian in origin, and that his mother had Russian blood. He had three sisters, he had informed her, all of them older than him and all of them married with families.

'It's a wonder I didn't grow up in terror of the female sex,' he told her with a grin as he handed her a generous helping of rhubarb fool. 'You wouldn't believe how much they bullied me.'

'No, I wouldn't,' Sorrel agreed darkly. 'They probably spoiled you to death.'

'Not a bit of it,' he assured her with a grin.

'What did they think of you coming over here to meet your English relatives?'

'Oh, they were all for it,' he told her promptly. 'In fact, they bet me that I'd probably go back with a...'

'With a what?' Sorrel asked him, curious not so much to know what he had been going to say, but the reason he had stopped so abruptly, giving her a look that was almost wary.

'An English wife,' he told her smoothly. So smoothly that she felt sure, for some reason, there was something he wasn't telling her.

But the wine had made her feel so woozy and relaxed that it was too much of an effort to hold on to the thought, and so she let it slip away, asking instead, 'Why should they think that?'

'Because that's what our original Llewellyn ancestor did. He was shipped over as a convict. He stole a loaf of bread. He was lucky it was only one loaf, otherwise he'd have been hanged and not transported, and that would have been the end. He was lucky in being chosen as an overseer by one of the colonists, mainly because he had some knowledge of farming methods—and after he'd served his seven years, he came back to England.'

'To find a wife?' Sorrel asked him, fascinated, but for some reason Val seemed reluctant to tell her any more.

'This is delicious,' he told her. 'Is there any more?'

'Yes. I'll get you some.' She stood up and then sat down again abruptly as her legs turned weak and wobbly and the room spun dizzyingly around her.

'Something wrong?'

'The wine. I've drunk too much of it... It's so strong.' And yet it didn't seem to have affected him, Sorrel noticed.

What she needed now was a couple of cups of strong coffee to sober her up, but when she tried to say as much the words became hopelessly tangled.

'I think you'd better just come and sit down by the fire,' Val told her, grinning at her.

'Not the fire,' Sorrel mumbled, 'fresh air.'

'In this weather? You're kidding!'

'Fire needs stoking. Upstairs as well,' Sorrel told him as she tried to stand up for a second time.

'Leave everything to me. Hey, it *has* gone to your head, hasn't it?' she heard Val saying in a voice that seemed to hold more of a suspicion of laughter than concern, and then she was swept up into his arms and deposited in front of the range in one of the two easy chairs, her head spinning so badly that she closed her eyes and moaned faintly. It was the wine, of course, and nothing to do with the wholly un-expected sensation of being picked up and carried in Val's arms, her head resting against his shoulder, her face turned into his skin so that her lips were almost touching the warm brown column of his throat. His skin fascinated her. She wondered woozily if he was tanned all over, and then blushed guiltily at the wantonness of her thoughts.

'Fire too hot?' she heard him asking her solicitously, and she opened her eyes reluctantly to find he was leaning over her, arms braced either side of her on the arms of the chair.

His shirt was open at the throat and she was sure she could see dark hair growing there. She had an odd squirmy feeling in her stomach—a sensation hitherto unknown to her. Andrew's torso was almost hairless, his skin very pale. He hated sunbathing and she remembered had only reluctantly removed his shirt when they had spent a day in Pembrokeshire, walking along the cliffs with Simon and Fiona during the summer. Her brother had laughed at him, Sorrel remembered, and although she knew she hadn't been meant to see it she had not missed the look of pity Fiona had given her.

Perhaps it was true that Andrew wasn't a very male man, certainly nothing like as male as Val. She gave a tiny shiver and, to her consternation, felt the hard, calloused weight of Val's palm against her forehead.

'Just checking to see if you had a fever,' he told her when her eyes opened wide.

'If anyone should have a fever, it would be you,' she told him crossly. 'Walking through that snow...'

'What would you have preferred me to do? Stayed in my car and frozen to death?'

The sensation of pain that struck her astounded her. She looked at him with confused, anguish-glazed eyes and suddenly his face came properly into focus and in his eyes she saw a predatory male look that made her body tense; then she blinked and it was gone, and she knew that she must have imagined it.

'Bed for you, I think,' she heard him saying wryly, 'before you pass out on me down here.'

'Won't pass out,' Sorrel told him indignantly. 'Can't—can't go to bed...not with you...'

She thought she heard him chuckle as he bent to pick her up, but her head was whirling round so much that she had to concentrate all her attention on that.

'If it bothers you that much, I can always doss down on the floor. It won't be the first time. I slept rough often enough when I was prospecting.'

'Prospecting?' Sorrel questioned him drowsily as he headed for the stairs. She could get quite used to being held in his arms, she decided woozily. There was something very pleasant about the sensation of him all around her. She liked the scent of his body, the maleness of him. It made her want to nestle and cuddle up against him.

'I'm a geologist, remember?' he told her.

The stairs were steep, but he reached the top barely out of breath, Sorrel recognised admiringly. She tried to imagine Andrew picking her up and carrying her to bed once they were married, but the image refused to form, and the wine-induced elation spinning through her body suddenly turned to dejection.

She *wanted* to marry Andrew, she reminded herself. And there was more to marriage than having a husband strong enough to pick her up in his arms. Andrew had different strengths...far more important strengths. But, dredge her brain though she did, she couldn't for some reason recall just what they were.

'This looks cosy,' she heard Val say appreciatively as he carried her into the bedroom.

One of the oil lamps stood in the deep window embrasure. She had left the curtains open, and outside the sky had cleared and the moon and stars were throwing glittering white light across the snow-covered hills.

'Looks as if it's freezing out there,' Val commented as he put her down on the bed. 'Of course, there's always the tried and true remedy of the old bolster down the middle of the bed,' she heard him musing.

'We don't have a bolster,' Sorrel told him. She felt deathly tired, her tongue somehow swollen and awkward in her mouth, making it difficult for her to enunciate clearly—nothing to do with her mother's elderberry wine, of course. Or was it? She tried to remember how many glasses she had had, and couldn't. She also tried to sit up, and groaned feelingly as the room spun round her.

She heard Val's chuckle, but it was too much of an effort to open her aching eyes and look at him.

Habit dictated that she get up and get ready for bed, but she felt so comfortable... The thought of the cold bathroom was less than appealing.

She felt Val move, his footsteps on the bare boards of the floor making the bed shake so that she could feel the tiny reverberations beating inside her skull and all the way down her spine.

'Well, Cousin Sorrel, which is it to be?' she heard him murmur against her ear. 'Are you going to condemn me to sleeping on the floor, or am I going to be allowed to share your bed?'

'Not *my* bed,' Sorrel told him crossly. 'Can't sleep on the floor, no spare bedding.' Her mother wouldn't be at all happy if she allowed their guest to spend a freezing cold night sleeping on bare boards, she thought muzzily. 'Have to share the bed...'

'Good girl.'

She winced, wishing he wouldn't speak so loudly. Her head was pounding and she gave a tiny moan.

'Don't worry. I won't tell the fiancé that we spent the night together.'

'Andrew would understand,' Sorrel told him quickly. She felt the bed move and opened her eyes. Val was leaning across her, easing down the bedclothes on the other side of the bed.

'Would he?' he asked her, his eyebrows lifting. 'I don't think *I* would in his shoes. Come on,' he added, watching as the expressions came and went muzzily in her eyes, her reactions slowed down by the effect of the wine. He had had no idea it would be quite so potent, nor that she would have such a weak head. All he had intended to do was to get her to relax a little, to stop her from being so uptight. 'Let's get you undressed and into bed.'

At the word 'undressed', Sorrel started to struggle away from him, danger signals flashing rapidly through her brain. Her hands clutched at her sweater, and Val laughed.

'Look, I promise you I have no designs on your virtue. I just thought you might be a little more comfortable without your sweater and jeans.'

He was right, of course, and his logical comment was no reason for her to suddenly suffer a rush of blood through her body that left every single part of it tingling in a most unnerving way.

'I can manage,' she told him fiercely, watching him warily, but he made no attempt to touch her, simply sitting back against the bottom of the bed and watching her.

'Where have I heard those words before?' he mocked her drily. 'Tell me, Sorrel, what does this fiancé of yours think of such stubborn independence?'

Stubborn? Her? She glowered at him.

'Andrew respects my need to be my own person,' she told him frigidly.

'Seems to me that respect seems to play a mighty important part in this relationship of yours.'

The sardonic twist of his lips brought her sharply back to awareness.

'Respect *is* very important in a marriage,' she told him.

'I agree, but surely not to the exclusion of everything else? Do you love him, Sorrel?' he asked her gently.

His question caught her off guard and made her focus determinedly on his face. There was no humour teasing the darkness of his eyes.

'Yes. Yes, of course I do,' she told him in a high, uncertain voice that wobbled a little, as though she wasn't quite as sure as she wanted to be.

'And when he kisses you, how does he make you feel?'

Her eyes widened in shock. There was no way he should be asking her that kind of question.

'Does he make you tingle all the way from the tip of your head down to your toes?' Val pressed, in a voice that suddenly seemed to be melting her bones, turning them into warm treacle. Or was it the mental image he had unwittingly drawn for her that was making her melt? An image of her body held in his arms, while his mouth . . .

She stared at him in utter confusion. It was the wine; it had to be. She had never in her life before experienced such wanton and thoroughly shocking desires.

'That's just romantic nonsense,' she told him stoutly. 'No one ever really feels like that.'

'Don't they?' His glance dropped to her mouth and Sorrel almost but not quite swayed towards him. The shock of her own illogical behaviour was enough to stop her, and to her relief Val got up off the bed, saying casually, 'I'll go downstairs and stoke up the boiler, if you're sure you can manage to get to bed by yourself. Don't worry, little cousin, you're perfectly safe. I have no intention of harming you or hurting you. By the look of you, by the time I come to bed you'll be fast asleep, dreaming the sweet, chaste dreams of innocent virgins. I'm looking forward to meeting this fiancé of yours. I don't think I've ever come across his like before.'

And the way he said it made Sorrel reflect crossly that it hadn't been a compliment.

She ought to have felt relief once he had gone. His absence ought to have galvanised her into getting ready for bed, while she had the privacy to do so, but she felt wholly reluctant to move. She thought of that cold, uninviting bathroom in contrast to the bedroom's delicious warmth... She snuggled down against the duvet with a faint sigh.

CHAPTER THREE

SOMEONE was moving her... lifting her... turning her...and Sorrel muttered protestingly in her sleep, conscious of a thread of laughter running through the soft words which rumbled against her body and yet which remained merely an alien sound. She felt a shaft of cool air touch her skin and protested again, wanting to burrow back into the warmth of the bed. There were sounds, familiar and yet distant, and somehow, like that rumbling voice, comforting. She sighed and relaxed back into her deep sleep, acknowledging with pleasurable voluptuousness the granting of her request to be restored to the burrow of warmth from which she had been removed.

Val, neatly folding the jeans and sweater he had removed from her, as well as the lace-edged thermal vest, smiled as he looked at her. She reminded him of a chestnut mare he had once owned: all delicate bones and high spirit. He had come to Wales with no fixed ideas on the family he was coming to find, and he had certainly had no intentions of embroiling himself in their personal affairs.

This was supposed to be a break, a chance to re-charge his batteries, a chance to get away from the relentless pressure of running a successful multi-million-dollar business.

He moved away from the bed, suddenly restless, remembering his sisters' teasing before he left Perth. Would he, like their ancestor, bring back a wife from Wales? Would a soft-spoken Welsh girl be able to achieve what their Australian sisters had not, and make him fall in love?

Love... What the devil was he thinking about? Love, the kind that could be shared by a man and a woman, wasn't something he had any personal experience of. Desire, yes, he knew all about that... but, little as he knew about love, he sus-pected it was a great deal more than the woman curled up fast asleep in the middle of the large bed. For all that she claimed she loved this fiancé of hers, she had no more awareness of what love was than a newborn kitten. What were her family thinking about? Why didn't they stop her... show her? He frowned and checked himself. She wasn't his responsibility. He was here on holiday, that was all. There was no point in getting involved. He looked at her sleeping face. How outraged and an-gry she had been to discover he was a man! He chuckled. It was a natural enough mistake, he sup-posed. The heat from the fire was making him sleepy, reminding him of how long it had been since he had last slept. He stretched, his body lithely muscled and honed to peak fitness by the hours he spent working outdoors, testing their boats. From geologist to boat builder; but he found a great deal more satisfaction in what he was doing now than he would ever have done in working for some large conglomerate. And he had been lucky; the money he had invested in that first small boatyard had multiplied over and over again. Perth was a boom town, full of people with money to spend, as the marinas full of new boats could testify. In the wake of the Americas Cup victory, sailing fever had gripped the country, and nowhere more so than on the Swan River town of Perth. Yes, he had caught the roller at the right moment, and for a while the success of his business had been enough to satisfy all his emotional needs. But there was more to life than work and financial success. He was thirty-five years old and as his sisters kept reminding him, not getting any younger. There were any number of sun-bronzed beautiful girls who hung around the marinas and the boatyards, who would be only too pleased to capture his attention, and had he been ten years younger he might have been interested. Strange, the changes the years brought. At twenty-five he had been stuck in the middle of the desert working his guts out as a geologist, with not a woman in sight.

There had been relationships at home, but none of them strong enough to survive his long absences, and they had ended without regret on either side.

Now it seemed he had reached an age where a pretty face and a willing body just weren't enough to stir more than cursory desire.

He shifted his weight restlessly from one foot to the other and looked at Sorrel. Why was she so set on marrying this fiancé of hers? A man whom, even if she herself didn't yet realise it, she didn't love. Out of loyalty? Out of fear of committing herself to a more dangerous relationship? Out of a deep-seated maternal need for children? Whatever the reason, she was making a mistake. A marriage needed far more than wishy-washy mutual respect as its foundations.

He had brought some logs upstairs with him, and he fed the fire with them, and then replaced the fireguard. He had already found the bathroom. No shower, of course, and freezing cold. Well, he had experienced worse. Much worse, he acknowledged humorously, looking at the pristine white linen of the sheets and the faded but beautiful patchwork quilt. The room held a faint scent of lavender and beeswax. It mingled pleasantly with the woody smell of the logs. He stripped off his jeans and woollen sweater and, unzipping his overnight bag, removed a towelling robe.

SORREL GRUMBLED in her sleep as she felt herself
being ousted from her deliciously warm spot in the
centre of the bed and gently levered on to cold linen
sheets. She shivered, her body heavy with stub-
bornness, not wanting to be moved. Sliding into the
bed beside her, Val discovered the reason why she
had been curled up in the middle of the bed. The
mattress dipped slightly in the centre.

Scrupulously aligning himself in his own half of
the bed, he too winced a little at the coldness of the
linen sheets, and reflected that he was beginning to
understand why some men wore pyjamas. Unfortunately he didn't possess any. As a token gesture
to modesty—Sorrel's and not his own, since he had
long ago lost any inhibitions he might once have felt
about his nudity—he had retained his briefs. His
feet were frozen and he just about managed to resist the temptation to slide them into the warm
space vacated by Sorrel's body. He chuckled a little to himself, contemplating her outrage were he to
warm them in the manner supposed to be traditional to married men. From what he had seen of
her body when he had undressed her, Sorrel's neatly
rounded bottom was shapely enough to tempt any
man.

Firmly suppressing the unwanted eroticism of his
thoughts, he closed his eyes. Less than ten minutes
later, he opened them again quickly. The sensation
of the soft, warm body burrowing against his own

so closely mirrored his own brief fantasy that at first he wasn't sure if he was merely imagining it...but, no, he acknowledged, grinning to himself, this was definitely real!

Obligingly he turned round to face Sorrel, and saw that she was deeply asleep. He supposed it was only natural that she should seek the warmth she had just left, and the dip in his centre of the bed had caused her to roll naturally against him.

He contemplated waking her up and pointing out to her that her behaviour was hardly in the spirit of her earlier remarks, and then acknowledged that to do so would be unnecessarily cruel. And, besides, it was very definitely a pleasure having her warmth cuddled up against him. He reached out to slip his arm around her and make himself more comfortable, and his fingers brushed against the silky fabric of her bra. He wondered what she normally wore in bed. A starched cotton nightdress with lots of Victorian lace and a high neck, perhaps; but certainly not her bra and panties. Deftly he reached for the catch of her bra and eased it away from her, telling himself that it couldn't be very comfortable for her wearing such a constricting garment while she slept, ignoring the fact that her satin bra was little more than a delicate wisp of fabric and that she herself seemed supremely unaware of any such constriction. He wondered what she would say if she woke up now and found herself virtually in his arms. She would be furious, of course. He could almost see her eyes darkening with temper now— and once he told her that *she* had been the one to cuddle up to *him* ... She wouldn't believe him, of course, not at first, and he would perhaps tease her a little, asking what her so-proper fiancé would think of such behaviour.

Suddenly he tensed. Of course! Now, why hadn't he thought of that before? She deserved better than her cold fish of a fiancé. She deserved to have a man who really appreciated her, who would cherish and love her. He had learned early from his elder sisters that even the most independent of women enjoyed being cosseted at times. And why not? Didn't all human beings enjoy a little bit of emotional spoiling when it came from someone they loved, and wasn't given in a patronising way, but out of loving and caring?

Against his chest, Sorrel sighed, her breath warm and sweet. Her head rested in the curve of his shoulder and he was scrupulously keeping their bodies from touching, even though every now and again Sorrel gave a restless sigh and pouted in her sleep, trying to cuddle closer to him—almost as though in some instinctive way she sensed his presence and wanted the physical contact with him. No woman who was genuinely in love with someone else would sleep so trustingly and innocently in his arms.

His body started to relax as tiredness caught up with him. Some time during the night, Sorrel had her way and their bodies meshed gently together, Val obligingly and instinctively moving his legs to make room for hers, his muscular thigh resting across her, imprisoning her within their sleeping embrace.

SORREL WOKE UP first, stretching languorously, blissfully warm and relaxed, and then abruptly she tensed, suddenly aware of the alien weight lying across her legs. She opened her eyes, blinking as she saw the warm brown flesh only centimetres from her face. An awful lot of unpleasant facts hit her at the same time.

Such as the fact that the delicious warmth bathing the front of her body came from the warm male flesh in such intimate contact with her own.

And the fact that the rhythmic rise and fall of that warm male chest was making her acutely aware of her bare breasts and the rather disturbing sensation caused by the unfamiliar roughness of a man's chest hair against her tender skin. And the fact that she was apparently imprisoned against that same male body by the solid muscled weight of the thigh thrown across her legs and the arm encircling her.

She moved experimentally. The light from the window held the cold, clear brightness of the snow outside, the fire had died down to a mere glow, and she wanted to escape before Val woke up and discovered how intimately they were entwined.

She moved again, wriggling impatiently. It was like trying to escape from a trap of solid rock. If she could just shift his leg . . .

She burrowed down under the bedclothes and put her hand on his thigh. Beneath her palms, the sensation of soft hair against firm, silky, skin-covered muscle was extraordinarily daunting. Her hands trembled crazily, as though imbued with a life of their own; a life which wantonly whispered to them to explore the solid sinew-roped limb beneath them, her fingertips almost stroking against his thigh instead of removing it.

'Mmm . . . nice . . .'

The soft purring words, the way his thigh flexed and then relaxed, as though mutely inciting her to caress it, almost made Sorrel jump out of her skin.

'You're . . . you're awake!' She wished she didn't sound so guilty, as though she had been doing something wrong.

She heard him laugh, a soft, satisfied sound that sent shivers trembling through her.

'I'd have to be made of stone to sleep through that . . . and to think I thought you didn't care,' Val murmured, deliberately teasing her.

Val had been awake for the last half-hour, too comfortable to move, drowsily wondering what she would do when she woke up and discovered that she had slept in his arms. Her attempts to stealthily put some distance between them had made him smile.

If he was any gentleman, he had told himself sternly, he would let her do it and tactfully pretend he knew nothing. But he wasn't a gentleman. Besides, it was too important to the plan he had formed before going to sleep. He had enjoyed sleeping so close to her. He couldn't remember the last time he had actually spent the whole night with a woman... and certainly never with one who was so innocently voluptuous. Too voluptuous and too innocent, he warned himself, remembering how he had felt when he'd first woken up and discovered that her naked breasts were nestled enticingly against his chest, her dark pink nipples buried in the crisp dark hair that grew there.

Instantly Sorrel snatched her hands away, her face burning. Surely he didn't think she had actually been trying to... to...'

'If you want to make love to me, there's no need to wait until I'm asleep,' he tormented her, and Sorrel, not hearing the humour in his voice, fell for the bait, trembling away from him.

'I *do not* want to make love to you. How dare you say such a thing?' she demanded, her face very pink.

The dark eyebrows quirked slightly, the bright light reflected off the snow showing the line of dark stubble on his chin.

'Seems to me that when a woman cuddles up to a man the way you did to me last night, and then starts stroking his . . .'

'I did nothing of the kind!' Sorrel protested furiously, sitting up in the bed and remembering too late that she was virtually naked.

The cold air in the bedroom raised a rash of goose-bumps on her skin and made her breasts tauten and lift, her nipples erect. She gave an inarticulate cry of consternation and slid hurriedly down under the sheet. The combined shock of the cold and her embarrassment had cleared her befuddled brain, and from the protection of the bed-clothes she snapped bitterly, 'And I suppose *you're* going to tell me that I *undressed* myself as well, are you, without even knowing I was doing it?'

'It was the wine,' Val told her shamelessly, sitting up himself and apparently uncaring of the cold. Unlike hers, his flesh did not react to it. He had the most marvellous tan, Sorrel reflected enviously. His chest was deep and broad, his body musky with its own special scent. The sheet slipped to his waist, revealing the supple strength of his spine. Hastily, she dragged her gaze away from him. Her head had started to pound, proof if she wanted it that she had had far too much to drink.

'You begged me to do it,' Val told her virtuously.

'Begged you to do what?' she demanded falteringly.

'Why, undress you, of course,' Val fibbed cheerfully. 'You said you didn't like sleeping in your clothes... and, being the gentleman that I am...'

He saw the militant sparkle in her eyes and veiled his own to hide his amusement. He was enjoying this game; and she deserved a little torment. After all, he had suffered enough of it himself, lying awake this morning, all too conscious of her delicious nakedness pressed up against him... all too aware that every breath she took was bringing those soft breasts of hers into closer contact with his body. And when she'd touched his thigh... He lifted his lids, and Sorrel, who had half expected to see mockery in his eyes, was astounded by the sudden sexual fierceness of the look he gave her. She literally shrank back from it, and demanded shrilly and dangerously, 'And my br—my underwear? I suppose you're going to tell me I asked you to remove that as well, are you?'

'You said it was digging into you,' Val assured her solemnly, and then added mischievously, 'Are you sure you and this fiancé of yours aren't lovers?'

A dark tide of colour burned up under Sorrel's skin: a mixture of fury, outrage and a very special female kind of embarrassment that sprang from the fact that she knew very well that she wasn't finding the memory of her physical contact with him anything like as abhorrent as she ought.

She knew that she ought to ignore him, that he was deliberately baiting her. She didn't have three brothers for nothing, after all, but even so she wasn't proof against her suddenly all too fevered imagination.

'Why?' she questioned him uneasily.

He saw the confusion and guilt in her eyes, and pounced on it.

'Well,' he said seriously, 'when you were begging me to take off your bra...' he bent his head and put his mouth to her ear, his fingers brushing aside the thick tendrils of her hair '...you whispered to me that you wanted to lie naked against me,' he told her outrageously. 'You said you wanted...'

'You're lying!' Sorrel gasped, pulling away from him, her face suddenly piteously white. She couldn't look at him, her whole body was gripped by tension. Surely she couldn't have done or said anything like that? Surely he was just teasing her, deliberately tormenting her? She could see that he found the whole situation amusing, while she...

'Oh, lord,' she moaned suddenly, her eyes burning. 'Andrew—'

Val, who had been on the point of relenting and admitting that he *was* tormenting her, changed his mind. It was for her own good, he assured himself virtuously, as he told her with as assuringly grave a manner as he could muster. 'Don't worry, I won't betray you. He need never know. How long is it exactly before you're getting married, by the way?' he asked her guilelessly.

Sorrel stared at him and started to tremble. 'What . . . what do you mean?' she asked him in a failing voice.

'Oh, nothing. Just that if you're going to make a habit of trying to seduce other men, it might be as well if . . .'

Trying to seduce, he had said. Relief coursed through her. For one appalling moment she had thought he was actually trying to imply that she. . .that they. . . But of course not. No matter how much elderberry wine she had drunk, she would surely have remembered something like that?

'I'd like to get dressed,' she told him stiffly.

'Go ahead. I folded your clothes and put them over there. All apart from your bra, that is,' he added musingly. 'Because we were already in bed when you begged me to take it off. Hang on a minute.' She saw his body move, and to her horror he produced her underwear from somewhere inside the bed, handing it to her with a smile that made her grit her teeth and curl her fingers into her palms. It

was either that or strangle him. How dared he lie
there and give her that dazzling smile, so completely the conquering, swaggering male? Lord, she
must have been mad to let him share the bed with
her. She ought to have locked and bolted the door
the moment she saw him... with him on the outside. Never mind if he *had* frozen to death!

'See,' he told her softly. 'I've even warmed it for
you.'

She couldn't help it; she blushed, openly and
vividly, and she blushed again when she heard him
laugh.

Furious both with him and herself, she said
fiercely, 'If you would just turn your back.'

'No need,' he assured her. 'After all, there's no
need for us to be shy with one another, is there? Not
after we've spent the night all wrapped up in each
other's arms.'

'I did not,' Sorrel swallowed and said hoarsely,
'That was a mistake... an accident. It...'

She gasped as he suddenly pushed back the
blankets and got out of bed, her rounded eyes filling with relief when she saw that he was wearing
briefs.

'Disappointed?' he teased her wickedly, grinning when she drew back with angry disdain. 'You
stay there. I'll go down and make us both a hot
drink. Or would you prefer me to stay?' he asked
suggestively.

Sorrel was horrified. 'No. No!'

Oh, please let her wake up and find that this was all some kind of horrible nightmare.

CHAPTER FOUR

'NOT still sulking, are you?' Val enquired. It was almost eleven in the morning. It hadn't taken more than a brief investigation of the conditions outside for both of them to acknowledge that they were snowbound, with no way of leaving the cottage until the snow thawed. Having prowled uneasily round the kitchen most of the morning, clattering pans and generally giving vent to her inner agitation, Sorrel was now sitting in front of the range, staring bitterly into space, wondering how on earth she had ever got herself into such a mess.

To make matters worse, she had the devil's own hangover—the sort that could probably only be cleared by either a hearty bout of tears or a good long walk, and it seemed unlikely that she was going to be able to indulge in either.

'Why?' she demanded trenchantly. 'Because you refused to seduce me?'

She was over her early-morning embarrassment and shock now. Reality had asserted itself and she was furious with herself for ever having been stupid enough to let him play on her fears so effortlessly. So she had *begged* him to undress her, had she? She ground her teeth impotently. Did he think she was a complete fool?

Oh, she could see what it was all about. Doubtless he found it all too amusing that she and Andrew had never been lovers—and she was pretty sure he was having a fine time tormenting her and making fun of her. It was obviously one way of alleviating the boredom of being cooped up with a twenty-four-year-old spinster who knew so little about men and sex that she could be fooled into thinking he had actually been her lover. Well, almost fooled into thinking it.

'The game's over, Cousin Val,' she told him grittily.

'If you say so,' he agreed obligingly.

'So you admit that it *was* a game,' Sorrel pounced, 'and that I *didn't*, that I didn't beg...ask you to take my clothes off?' Her face was red by the time she had finished, but she was determined to stand her ground.

'Can't you remember?' Val asked her softly.

Damn him, he had caught her out again, and the infuriating thing was that she *couldn't* remember—not a damn thing apart from a delicious feeling of warmth and blissful security.

'I may be a raw colonial, but in my part of the world we never discuss what a lady—er—may or may not have said in an intimate situation.'

There he went again, deliberately making fun of her. Any intimacy between them had been caused by an accidental physical proximity and nothing else.

'Will you tell your fiancé—Andrew—about sleeping with me?' he asked her casually.

Sorrel looked at him, her skin growing uncomfortably warm.

'If the subject comes up,' she told him uneasily, trying to imagine herself saying casually to Andrew during one of their dates, Oh, and by the way, you remember when I was up at the old farm with Val? Well, we slept together. Nothing serious—he just took off virtually all my clothes and held me in his arms, threw his thigh across me and...

'If it comes up?' The dark eyebrows rose in that now familiar quirk. 'You mean, it may not? Hell, if my woman had spent three days alone with another man, I'd damn well want her to account for every single second of her time.'

'Andrew and I trust one another,' Sorrel told him loftily. 'He knows that I wouldn't... that...'

'Perhaps he believes that because he doesn't want to make love to you, no other man does either,' Val suggested quietly.

It was too much. Too close to home for comfort, too cutting and cruel after his earlier remarks to her about her pleas to him to undress her. She wondered uneasily if she was wrong, after all, and if she had... But no, surely not? She started to panic, wishing she could remember, wishing she hadn't drunk so much wine, wishing she had never allowed herself to be persuaded to come up here. Wishing that Valentine Llewellyn had in fact been Valerie.

Her body burned uncomfortably as she wondered if perhaps she did have much stronger sexual urges than she had always believed, if perhaps those urges had betrayed her into... Her throat had gone very dry. She swallowed hard, and Val, taking pity on her, said calmly, 'You said something about some family diaries. Do you think I could have a look at them?'

Sorrel seized on the excuse to escape from him. The kitchen had suddenly become unbearably claustrophobic. If they had to stay here another night, and it looked very much as though they might, then there was no way she was going to... Her mind shied away from the thought.

She would sleep downstairs on one of the chairs—anything, anything rather than risk sharing that bed with him again.

She dallied over getting the diaries, but the cold in the rest of the house drove her back to the kitchen.

Stiltedly at first, and then more easily, she explained to him the family tradition. She had been fascinated by the diaries ever since she had first been allowed to read them. It was several years since she had last looked at them, and as she handed the first one to Val she was surprised to see how reverently and gently he touched it. He would touch and hold a woman with that same reverent care, that same gentleness that came only from strength, that same...

She had to swallow again, trying not to remember how impatient Andrew had always been over what he termed her sentimentality about the diaries. He claimed that they should be sold, that they were of great value. He couldn't understand why the family insisted on keeping them. She had never told him that she was maintaining the family tradition and keeping one herself, and it startled her to hear Val saying quietly, 'When did you first start writing in yours?'

She looked at him in surprise.

'How did you know?'

'It wasn't hard,' he told her with a smile. 'I guess you'd have been about eleven or twelve...a girl trembling on the brink of womanhood, sensitive...too sensitive, perhaps.'

He saw too much, was too perceptive. It frightened her in some way.

'Why are you doing it, Sorrel?' he asked her softly. 'Why the hell are you marrying a man you don't love?'

'I *do* love him,' she retaliated. 'You don't understand. Some people don't need passion or excitement or...'

'Desire,' he murmured, suddenly standing far too close to her. 'That's not true, Sorrel. All of us need all of those things, and if you believe any differently you're short-changing Andrew, and even worse, you're short-changing yourself.'

'You don't understand,' she said shakily. 'I don't *want* those things. I want my marriage to be safe.'

'Safe?' His eyebrows shot up. 'Ye gods! You tell me you don't want any of the things that a marriage needs for a strong foundation, and then you tell me you want it to be safe. What is it you're so frightened of, Sorrel? Loving someone, losing them—or is it something within yourself you fear?'

He saw the panic in her eyes and knew he had scored a home point.

Without Sorrel being aware of it, he had reached out and circled her wrist within his fingers. Now they stroked softly against the frantic pulse beating in her wrist. Her blood seemed to take to the rhythmic movement, there was an odd roaring in her ears, like the sound of the sea inside a shell.

'What is it that makes you so frightened, Sorrel?' he pressed. 'What?' She was looking at him, but he sensed that she wasn't seeing him. Some kind of inner conflict was holding her in its grip, her eyes were glittering with tension, the pupils almost black.

'Of losing control, of being caught up in something I can't control, of...' She gave a deep shudder and focused on him, going abruptly silent.

'I see.' He was still stroking her wrist, almost absently, or so it seemed, and yet his movements had a calming effect on her racing pulse, whereas before... She didn't want to think about those tiny shivers he had sent racing up her arm, that odd coiling sensation that had made her ache inside.

'When you say you're frightened of losing control, I take it you mean the kind of loss of control that comes when a man and woman make love...really make love?'

Her eyes reflected her shock at his acuteness. He smiled at her and said gently, 'It wasn't so hard to deduce, you know. A woman as beautiful as you, as made for love as you, could only remain virginal by an extreme effort of will. What happened, Sorrel? Did someone hurt you? A man...'

He was way off the right track, and she shook her head swiftly.

'No, nothing like that...'

A tiny dart of cold dread touched his heart, and his fingers stopped soothing and gripped her wrist.

'Sorrel, you aren't by any chance trying to tell me that you...that you prefer...'

'No!'

He wasn't sure if he liked the relief that washed over him.

'What is it, then?' he asked her, genuinely puzzled.

Suddenly Sorrel wanted to tell him, although she couldn't really understand why. She didn't like him or trust him, he made fun of her, teased her and taunted her. He was turning her whole world upside-down, and yet she had the extraordinary feeling that she could stand in front of him and lay her soul bare to him without having him judge or mock her.

'It was when I was eleven,' she told him shakily. 'I was staying here with Gran and Gramps. I'd gone out for a walk. It was a hot sunny day at the end of summer...' Her eyes clouded over, and Val sensed that she was not seeing him but looking back into the past.

'There's a special place almost half-way up the hillside. You can't see it until you're virtually on top of it. A sort of gully, with scree and a couple of scrubby trees. There's a pool at the bottom and the sides are covered with heather. I was going to stop there for my sandwiches, only when I got there...' she swallowed hard, 'there was someone there already. A couple, actually. They were making love.' Her throat felt raw, as though a bone was scraping it, her voice revealing her torment. 'I'd never seen people together like that before. Both of them were naked...oblivious...I saw him touch her breasts...kiss them. At first when she cried out I thought he was hurting her. I knew I ought to go away, at any moment they could look up and see me, but it was as though there was only the two of them left on earth. A flying saucer could have landed and they would have been oblivious to it. Especially the woman. It was as though she was formless clay and he was moulding her...fashioning her into something for his own private pleasure.'

Her voice had become strained and tight, her whole body expressing her tension. 'It frightened me. She was so...so vulnerable. I ran away then. I couldn't bear to see any more. The whole thing terrified me, and I felt guilty because I knew I should never have watched, but I couldn't seem to help myself.'

Val, with certain memories of his own of making love out in the open beneath a summer sky, hid his own amusement and concentrated instead on her anguish. He could well understand how frightening it might be to a too sensitive child-woman to witness the full extent of a woman's passion. He could even understand that she might feel threatened by it, because she had viewed it as a child, and not as an adult; had seen the woman's total subjugation of a need which, to her untutored eyes, seemed to be controlled by the man, not realising that he had probably been as much in thrall to desire as she had been.

'And it's because of that that you're marrying Andrew?' he asked her gently. 'Because...'

'I know it's silly, but the thought of ever feeling like that terrifies me.'

He could see that. Her teeth had literally started to chatter with shock, making her body go cold.

'I know that with Andrew it won't be like that. It won't feel like that,' she told him with painful honesty.

He waited for a moment and then asked her quietly, 'Hasn't it occurred to you that to have a sexual relationship *without* desire can be just as painful...just as hurtful?'

'Thousands of women have done,' she reminded him. 'Women who were married to men chosen by their families.'

'Women who were never allowed to acknowledge their right to their own sexuality,' Val told her grimly. 'Hell, Sorrel...think—think what you're *doing* to yourself. When you saw that couple making love, you saw them with the eyes of a child. Your own burgeoning awareness of yourself as a woman distorted your reaction to it.'

'No!' Sorrel told him tightly, pulling away from him. 'I don't want to talk about it any more. I don't want to feel like that...I don't want...' She started to shiver and she heard Val curse as he came towards her.

'You know your trouble don't you?' he told her as he almost pushed her down into a chair. 'You've got a darn sight too active an imagination. It isn't just women who lose control in the act of love. Men do as well.'

'Not in the same way,' Sorrel told him through chattering teeth. 'I don't want to talk about it any more, Val. You don't understand.'

'Oh, but I do,' he told her with a grimness that might have made warning signals of danger flash through her brain if she hadn't been so caught up in her fear. 'Tell me something,' he asked her, turning his back on her, 'when you watched them making love, was it just fear that you felt, Sorrel?'

Her whole body tensed, her mind desperately seeking an escape route. How could he know about that shaming surge of sensation that had made her body go hot and light? That aching feeling between her thighs that had made her touch herself in shocked fear?

'Yes,' she lied frantically, 'just fear.'

'Mm. Well, I don't think you really do have anything to fear, then.' He turned round suddenly, looking directly into her eyes, his own cool and unreadable.

For some odd reason, instead of reassuring her, his words hurt her. Was he saying that there was something wrong with her?

'I should stop worrying about it if I were you,' he told her casually. 'And perhaps you're right about marrying Andrew.'

'I am,' she told him stonily, suddenly feeling thoroughly out of charity with him and resenting him for somehow or other tricking her into giving him confidences she had never shared with anyone...nor even imagined herself doing. It made her feel very vulnerable that he should know so much about her, and she trembled a little, bitterly regretting that she had ever confided in him.

'Is there a spade in the outhouse?'

The question startled her.

'Yes. I should think so.'

'Good. I think I'll have a go at clearing the yard. Lucky I stopped to buy a pair of boots once it started to snow.'

Did he realise how much she needed to be on her own to gather together her scattered thoughts and composure? No, surely not? She risked an upward glance into his face. Hard-boned and very male, it made her shiver a little and marvel at the madness that had made her confide in him so unwisely.

'If I'm not back by the time it gets dark, you'd better send out a search party,' he joked.

Sorrel gave him a wan smile. All she wanted to do was get him out of the house. Her teeth ached with the tension inside her. She had never met anyone who caused her to have so many contrary emotional reactions. It seemed impossible that one mere man could cause her such turbulence... Unless... unless her fear of giving herself in the act of sexual intimacy sprang from some deep inner knowledge of a vulnerability so intense that she had deliberately hidden it from herself. Had deliberately only ever allowed herself to date men who could not have the kind of effect on her that made her vulnerable. Men like Andrew, and not men like Val.

She watched him walk outside and cross the yard. The snow lay deep in drifts against the stone wall that marked the boundary between the yard and the land. She picked up one of the diaries and tried to concentrate on it, ignoring the sounds of activity from the yard, but the written words couldn't hold her attention. She told herself it was because she had read them before and had nothing to do with the fact that Val was outside.

She turned to her tapestry, but she couldn't concentrate on that either. Restlessly she toured the kitchen. They were having soup for lunch by mutual consent, conserving their food just in case Simon couldn't get through, and then for dinner there was the steak chilled in the pantry. She went to the window, giving in to the urge that drove her. Val had cleared a surprisingly large piece of the yard. She watched him working. Her eyes followed the controlled movement of his body. He was used to working outside, his muscles supple. He glanced up and saw her, and to cover her embarrassment at being caught watching him, she indicated that she was making him a hot drink.

Caught in her own trap, she filled the kettle and, while she waited for it to boil, on some impulse she didn't want to analyse she pulled on her own wellingtons and her jacket, before preparing the drink.

It was cold outside, the icy air stinging her skin and hurting her lungs until they grew used to it, but despite the cold there was something invigorating about being outside, something magical in the crisp unbroken whiteness of the landscape, something oddly exhilarating in feeling as if they were the only two people in the world.

She handed Val the mug of chocolate she had made, careful to avoid any physical contact between them, her face suddenly growing hot as she realised that the accidental touching of their hands was hardly likely to be important after she had spent the night virtually naked in his arms.

'Too cold for you?' Val asked her, noting the sudden surge of colour.

'No. I like the snow. There's something special about it.'

'Yes...like it's cold,' Val agreed, turning his back on her. Before she could guess what he intended, a soft snowball hit her gently, splattering against the front of her jacket.

Unrepentant, he stood grinning at her, almost daring her in the way that the twins and Simon did.

'You asked for this,' she warned him. 'I'll have you know that I won the snowballing championship at school three years running.'

'So, show me,' Val taunted her with another grin, ducking just in time to avoid the first missile she hurled at him.

After that the snowballs flew fast and furious, no quarter given and none asked. Sorrel had the experience and a good eye, Val had the advantage of his height and strength, and soon both of them were liberally covered in white blobs. Grimacing as she brushed snow out of her hair, Sorrel started to edge towards the wall. If she could get behind it she would have protection from Val's aim, and somehow would stockpile enough ammunition to wipe that grin off his face and show him just what being a Welsh Llewellyn meant.

She was almost there when he suddenly realised what she was doing, lunging towards her and throwing her to the ground with a rugby tackle that made the breath fly out of her body.

The snow cushioned her and she collapsed into a drift, spluttering with a mixture of laughter and chagrin.

'Get off me. You weigh a ton,' she complained.

Val had followed her down into the drift, and now the weight of his body was keeping her there. A pleasurable weight, it had to be admitted; a too pleasurable weight, the startling reaction of her body suddenly told her, making her struggle and push against his chest.

He seemed oblivious to her urgent desire to break free, sliding his arm companionably round her and looking down into her eyes.

'I've heard that making love in the snow is something that has to be experienced to be believed,' he murmured softly.

Instantly her body tensed. He was tormenting her again, and her indignant expression told him that she was fully aware of his tactics.

'You mean to say you *haven't* done?' she taunted back, still struggling to break free. 'You do surprise me.'

'We could experience it together,' he told her, shocking her into immobility, her eyes focusing on his with disbelief.

'Best way to overcome a trauma is to exorcise it,' he added. His mouth seemed to touch her throat, the contact so brief that she couldn't be sure if she had imagined it.

'Would you like that, Sorrel?' he whispered against her ear, his breath stirring her hair, making her feel far too warm. 'Would you like me to make you burn and melt . . . to . . .'

What was he trying to do to her? And after what she had told him... Let that be a warning to her, she thought bitterly, to never, ever trust a man.

'Stop it,' she demanded, pushing angrily against his chest. 'I don't know what kind of game you think you're playing, but—'

'Who says it's a game?' he murmured, and this time she was sure that his lips *were* caressing the soft skin below her ear. It took all her energy not to shiver in reaction. 'Spending the night with a desirable woman curled up naked in his arms has a certain effect on a man's imagination . . . not to mention his body,' he told her wryly, 'and if you will keep throwing yourself into my arms . . .'

Her body sagged in relief. He was teasing her, after all. For one moment she had actually thought he was serious, but it was just another game. Another teasing mockery of her susceptibility.

'As I remember it, *you* were the one who did the throwing,' she pointed out firmly. 'And as for your imagination . . . remember, I'm a woman with a very low sex drive. A virgin.'

'I'm prepared to make allowances,' he told her magnanimously.

Sorrel shot him a suspicious look.

'You enjoy doing this, don't you?' she demanded bitterly. 'You just love making fun of me, tormenting me...'

'Put it down to the fact that as a child I was bullied to death by three older sisters,' he told her. 'I have to get my own back.'

'Well, not with me,' Sorrel assured him.

He was laughing down at her, his eyes crinkling at the corners, and she had a sudden sensation of falling free of the earth and hanging in space. It made her blink and go quite pale.

Val saw her change colour and frowned.

'Come on,' he said abruptly, getting up and hauling her to her feet. 'Otherwise we'll freeze. Now that would be a sight come the thaw, wouldn't it?' he mused wickedly. 'The two of us clasped in one another's arms. Frozen together.'

'It's not a sight I would find at all diverting,' Sorrel assured him.

They were half-way towards the porch door when he suddenly stopped and said thoughtfully, 'That couple you saw. He must have been a brave man.'

She stared uncertainly at him, a certain glint in his eyes warning her that he wasn't through tormenting her.

'A hot day...the sun... It isn't very pleasant having a burned backside.'

Sorrel pulled away from him and hurried into the house. Her face was glowing from more than the cold as she bent to remove her wellingtons. She was a fool to let him do it to her. It was evident to anyone with the intelligence of a two-year-old how much he enjoyed baiting her. She wanted to crawl away and die, but Val wasn't going to let her. He was standing beside her, watching her gravely.

'That was some instant education you got, wasn't it?' he said quietly. 'I'm sorry if my teasing upset you. I guess I'm just not used to being around women as innocent and...'

'Sexless as me,' Sorrel finished bitterly for him. 'There's no need to apologise. I should have realised I was out of my depth.'

And, with that, she stalked past him and slammed into the kitchen.

Why, oh, why was it that in each of their encounters he managed to come off best?

CHAPTER FIVE

THROUGHOUT the afternoon, Sorrel kept giving surreptitious glances out of the kitchen window, hoping to see signs of a thaw, even while experience told her that, if anything, there was likely to be a further drop in the temperature.

Val appeared to be deeply engrossed in the diaries. After lunch he had insisted on doing the washing up and making them both large mugs of coffee, and now, watching him covertly, Sorrel was struck by the air of complete relaxation and ease which he wore. For a man used to an outdoor life, he seemed able to adapt to being forcibly cooped up inside extremely well.

Both her father and Simon hated any kind of inactivity, her father in particular, and Sorrel didn't think she'd ever seen him sit down and read anything other than farming journals. If he had been up here, by now he would be driving her mother mad, prowling round the kitchen, constantly going to check on the weather, grumbling and complaining.

Andrew, on the other hand, was not a physically active man—a fact which was perhaps betrayed by his rather slender frame. At school he had hated sports, and now his whole life revolved around his bookshop. His only real hobby was attending various antiquarian book sales and mingling with other aficionados whose tastes matched his own.

Quite often when she went round to his flat to spend the evening with him, he would be busy reading something he had just bought, and Sorrel had learned to take a small tapestry with her or one of her designs so that she had something to occupy herself with.

Unlike Val, Andrew rarely offered to wash up or help her prepare the meals she cooked for them. He was an only child and his widowed mother had spoilt him. He still went to see her every Sunday to take her to church and have lunch with her. Sorrel had occasionally joined him on these visits, but she sensed that Andrew's mother had never really liked her.

She had a god-daughter whose name she invariably mentioned in Sorrel's presence, remarking fondly on what a lovely girl she was, how domesticated and gentle, and what a wonderful wife she would make. Sorrel suspected that Mrs James would much prefer Andrew to be marrying her god-daughter.

She glanced at the window again and saw with a sinking heart that it had started snowing. Val, whom she could have sworn had never raised his head from the diary he was reading, remarked conversationally, 'From the look of the sky, it seems as though it's going to be a good while yet before it lets up.'

Which meant that it could be heaven knew how long before they could leave the farm. Tiny tremors of alarm sped down her spine, making her say sharply, 'Since when have you been an expert on Welsh weather?'

She bit her lip, regretting her irritation. The last thing she wanted to do was to betray to him how nervous and vulnerable she felt. She had seen already how much he enjoyed teasing her.

She waited tensely for him to make some taunting comment, but instead he simply closed the diary and got up, stretching lithely; she could hear the faint crack of his bones beneath the pressure of his luxurious stretch. If one looked at him with purely dispassionate eyes, as a male animal he really was superb, she acknowledged shakily. A woman would have to be carved in marble not to be aware and appreciative of that fact.

'I'm not trying to be an alarmist,' he told her quietly. 'And you're right, of course, I don't know the first thing about local weather conditions here, but I do know a snow-heavy sky when I see one.

You said the arrangement was that we'd stay up here for three days until the twins went back to university. As a precaution, and only as a precaution, it occurs to me that it might be a good idea if we started rationing the food a little.' He looked towards the window. 'If this keeps up, will your brother be able to get through?'

Sorrel went and joined him. In the yard, the flakes fell thick and heavily, but outside, where the land was exposed to the wind, they were being driven into drifts, whirling in some mad dance that was slowly obliterating the landscape.

'No,' she admitted honestly. 'He'll try, of course.'

She bit her lip again, knowing how worried her family would be. Of course they would do everything they could to get through to them. This wouldn't be the first time the farm had been cut off by heavy snows.

'I reckon we're all right for fuel. I found another four sacks of logs in one of the barns while I was looking for a spade, and there's an outhouse with some boiler fuel in it. It might be an idea to bring some of the logs in and dry them off a bit. They could be damp. So at least we can keep warm.'

'And there's plenty of oil for the lamps,' Sorrel told him.

'Food? How much of that do we have?' His eyebrows rose interrogatively.

'A fair amount of staples—tea, coffee, flour, dried milk. And there's always an emergency supply of tins in one of the cupboards. Dad or Simon come up here to check the place over pretty regularly.'

'We'd better just check and see what there is.'

A horrible hollow sensation made Sorrel feel distinctly shaky. She had been so caught up in her own emotional problems that she hadn't given any thought to the practical aspects of their incarceration.

Val followed her over to the old-fashioned oak cupboards beneath the dresser. She kneeled down to open the door, for some reason acutely conscious of him as he kneeled beside her. It was ridiculous to let him unnerve her like this. And why? Because through a series of misunderstandings and quirks of fate they had ended up spending the night together.

It hadn't been a quirk of fate that had been responsible for the removal of her clothes, Sorrel reminded herself angrily, wondering why, when she had been asleep at the time, she should have this disconcertingly real sensation of remembering how those long, deft fingers had felt moving against her skin.

Stop worrying about it, she cautioned herself. It obviously meant nothing to him that they had virtually slept naked in one another's arms, and he was deriving a huge amount of amusement from her own embarrassment and anger over what had happened, so the best thing she could do was to put it out of her mind.

And yet, as she reached into the cupboard, she tensed for a second, remembering that now inexplicable feeling she had had that she could confide in him, turn to him, trust him.

Trust him? She must have been mad! Her face burned as she remembered with self-loathing how many of her inner fears she had revealed to him.

'Is there anything in there?'

His words made her start and realise that she was so completely wrapped up in her thoughts that she hadn't made any attempt to check. She felt inside the cupboard.

'Yes. There are some tins at the back here.'

'Right, let's get them out and see what we've got.'

It proved to be quite a worthwhile haul. Five tins of new potatoes, four of a particular brand of minced beef that Simon loved, half a dozen tins of soup and three of vegetables.

'Looks as though we're in luck.'

Sorrel noticed him checking on the condition of the tins as she handed them to him.

'Well, at least we're not going to starve,' he told her. 'With these, plus the stuff you brought with you, we should be able to keep going for quite a while. How long do you think we're likely to be snowed in for?'

'It's hard to say,' Sorrel told him honestly. 'Normally when we get snow at this time of the year, it doesn't stay very long, but the temperature's still below freezing.'

'Umm... It's a pity you didn't think to bring a radio with you,' he commented dispassionately. 'What do you think your family will do once they realise they can't get through to us?'

'Dad and Simon will do their best, but they won't take any unnecessary risks. It isn't worth it. A snow plough will probably clear the main road, but I doubt if it will come up the lane.'

'Well, it looks as though we'll just have to sit it out and wait,' Val pronounced. Oddly, he didn't seem at all perturbed at the idea and, having replaced the tins in the cupboard, he asked Sorrel, 'Has anyone ever thought of writing a history of the family? With the help of those diaries...'

'Not really. None of us has that kind of talent.'

'One of my sisters is a writer. I'm sure she'd be very interested in seeing them.'

'I don't think Mum and Dad would want to send them out of the country,' Sorrel began to tell him.

'No, I wasn't suggesting that. Nadia and her husband have been promising themselves a visit to Europe for some time. The only thing that's stopping them is the thought of being away from the twins.'

He saw Sorrel's look and grinned. 'It isn't only *your* branch of the family that's got them, you know. Nadia and Rosy are twins, and then Nadia has twin boys, James and Nathan, and Gwen has a full house... a pair of each.'

'What?'

He laughed again at Sorrel's expression. 'You should have heard her when she discovered that her second pregnancy was twins as well... Mike said he'd never heard such language.'

They sounded like a close family—much like her own—and Sorrel felt a brief stirring of curiosity about them. Because the relationship between Val's family and her own was not a close one, she had not hitherto thought of them as a family, but now suddenly she did. It was odd to think of a part of their family living on the other side of the world.

'What made you decide to try and trace us?' she asked him curiously.

He got up, helping her to her feet at the same time. The warm grip of his fingers made her tingle, and she snatched her hands back.

'Perhaps I had a premonition that I had a very beautiful distant cousin who was about to make a big mistake in her life and—'

'If you're referring to my marriage to Andrew,' Sorrel interrupted him indignantly, 'it is not a mistake.'

'No, it isn't,' Val agreed, suddenly grim. 'To call it a mistake suggests that you don't know what you're getting yourself into, but you do. Dammit, Sorrel, you're deliberately trapping yourself into a relationship which will give about as much pleasure as... For heaven's sake, can't you *see* what you're doing?' he asked her explosively.

'Yes. This marriage is what I want. All right, so it might not appeal to you, but I'm not you, Val. I have different needs ... different wants—'

'You don't know the first thing about what you need or want,' he interrupted her bluntly.

Sorrel compressed her lips and glared at him.

'That is the most chauvinistic thing I've ever heard. Just because I'm a woman, you assume that I'm not capable of knowing my own mind.'

'Rubbish!' The curt objection silenced her. 'That is about the most specious argument I've ever heard. If you really want my opinion, then I'll tell you that I consider women to be far stronger than men...far more capable of knowing what they want from life...far better adjusted to cope with life's knocks. Mature women, that is, but you aren't mature, are you, Sorrel? You're still an eleven-year-old child clinging to a fear that you should have outgrown years ago.'

'That's not true.'

'Isn't it?' he challenged her.

Sorrel had had enough. She would have given anything to be able to turn her back on him and storm out, but there was nowhere to go other than an empty cold room, or upstairs to the bedroom. She wriggled uncomfortably, suddenly aware that she didn't want to go up there, where she might fall prey to the odd sensations of warmth and pleasure that were all rooted in her body's awareness of how much it had enjoyed its physical contact with Val.

'It's a subject on which we'll just have to agree to differ,' she told him with as much dignity as she could muster.

'Coward,' he taunted her, and Sorrel mentally cursed his three elder sisters and the knowledge they had given him about the mental processes and emotions of the female sex.

'You're a fine one to talk,' she threw at him. 'Thirty odd, and still single.'

'Not because I see myself as a perennial bachelor,' he assured her, surprising her. She had decided that he must be the kind of man who enjoyed having a changing parade of women through his life, and that he did not have the emotional stability or desire to commit himself to one woman.

'No?' she enquired sarcastically. 'Secretly you're just dying to settle down and produce heaven alone knows how many sets of twins, is that it?'

'Don't knock it,' he advised her, his Australian accent suddenly exaggerated. 'Lady, that's exactly what I plan to do.'

'You're planning to get married?' For some reason she was shocked. 'You're engaged?'

'I don't believe in engagements. Once you've found the person you want to spend your life with, there shouldn't be any need for time to think about it. How long have you been engaged?'

She glowered at him and said stiffly, 'Two years.'

His eyebrows rose. 'Not exactly an enthusiastic lover, is he?'

'I've already told you . . .'

'You're not lovers? Yes, I know. Wake up, Sorrel, before it's too late.'

ALTHOUGH she told herself that he had simply been getting at her, Sorrel couldn't help reflecting on what he had said as she worked on her tapestry. Val was still immersed in the diaries. It had stopped snowing and the sun had come out, but Sorrel doubted if the temperature had risen.

'Frost tonight,' Val remarked laconically. 'I'd better go and light a fire in the bathroom. We'll need it.'

Sorrel kept her head bent over her work, but her hands trembled and she stabbed her finger quite painfully with her needle. If he thought for one moment that they were spending another night together...

She heard him go upstairs and guessed from the sounds from above that he was cleaning out the fire. She had to admit that if she *had* to be snowed up with a strange man, then Val at least projected an aura of self-confidence and practicality that made the ordeal seem less intimidating. She tried to imagine how Andrew would have reacted in the same circumstances, and had to acknowledge that her fiancé would not have been a tower of strength. Then she frowned, annoyed with herself for comparing Andrew to Val, and even more annoyed with herself for finding Andrew wanting.

It was not his fault he wasn't the kind of man a woman could lean on if she wanted to. She had not chosen him for his macho male characteristics, after all. She had chosen him because... Her needle slipped and she cursed mildly under her breath, not wanting to admit that she was suddenly not quite sure why she had chosen him.

That was Val's fault, for filling her mind with all sorts of doubts. Self-doubts, she acknowledged painfully, doubts that had no right to be there. She was not the sort of person, who, having only embarked on a course, liked to be deflected from it. Marriage, to her, was a serious responsibility. Once married, she would have made a commitment to Andrew for all of her lifetime, and she wondered shakily why such a thought should suddenly induce a feeling of panic and dread.

Val came downstairs with the previous night's ashes, which he left in the porch.

'Snow's drifted half-way up the outside wall,' he told her briefly when he came back with fuel and logs. 'So much for clearing the yard this morning.'

'The fresh air will have done us both good,' Sorrel told him absently. 'And at this time of the year, at least once the thaw sets in, the snow should disappear quickly.'

'Before that fiancé of yours discovers you've been here alone with me,' he teased her.

Immediately anger flashed in her eyes.

'I've already told you, Andrew will understand the situation. You make it sound as though I deliberately sneaked away to... to...'

'To sample the pleasure *he* can't give you?' Val suggested.

'What? No! That wasn't what I meant at all, and you know it.'

She heard him whistling as he went upstairs—an unfamiliar tune, but one which held undertones of some kind of triumphal march.

Oh, wouldn't she just love to bring him down a peg or two!

IT WAS ONLY sensible that they should use up the
fresh food first, keeping the tins as an emergency
reserve.

The low temperature and the cold box supplied
by her mother were ensuring that their supplies were
kept fresh. She was going to cook chicken for dinner, casseroling it in the range.

'Smells good,' Val commented appreciatively.
'Anything I can do?'

Sorrel shook her head. The chicken would virtually cook itself; she had filled the casserole with
vegetables and thickened it with some of the flour.
If there had been any of the elderberry wine left . . .
She blenched a little at the memory of it. Her
mother had only put a couple of bottles in with the
supplies, saying that Valerie might appreciate a
glass of something to drink after dinner. Sorrel
doubted that her mother had anticipated them dis-
posing of both bottles in one go!

As the sky grew dark and the atmosphere inside
the kitchen somehow became more intimate, she
could feel her stomach muscles clenching. It was no
exaggeration to say she was dreading what lay
ahead. Of course, she intended to make it clear to
Val that tonight was not going to be a repeat of
what had happened last night.

The tension which was gripping her seemed to be
having no effect on Val whatsoever. He ate his evening meal with every evidence of enjoyment while

she—while she could barely force down a mouthful.

'Not hungry?' he asked her, watching her push her chicken around on her plate.

'There's something we need to discuss,' she told him firmly, taking a deep breath. 'About the... sleeping arrangement.'

His eyebrows rose, inviting her to continue.

'I'm sure that both of us can see that it wouldn't be...wise to—' Oh, heavens, why was it that, however she phrased it, her words were going to imply an intimacy that just hadn't existed? 'To both sleep in the one bed...so I think that tonight you should have the quilt and sleep down here, and I'll have the bed, and then tomorrow I'll sleep downstairs...and with luck by then it might have started to thaw.'

'Want some coffee?' Val asked her cheerfully, getting up and collecting her plate as well as his own.

Well, at least she had said what she wanted to say, and thankfully he hadn't made the kind of outrageous comments she had expected.

She should have felt relieved, because she had been working herself up to this moment all evening, but if anything she felt more tightly strung up than before. She wanted to ask Val if he was in agreement with her suggestion, but sensed that to do so would be to imply that somehow or other she wasn't as sure of herself as she should be, and so she kept silent.

Val whistled as he washed up, and then settled quite happily back to his reading until at about ten o'clock he started to ask her about her grandparents and the kind of life they would have lived up here.

As she answered his questions, Sorrel discovered that gradually she was relaxing. He had a way of drawing people out, she recognised, of being so interested in what they were saying that it was easy to talk to him, and almost before she knew it it was eleven o'clock.

'I . . . I think I'll go up now,' she told him huskily. 'There's plenty of hot water for a bath if you want one, the range heats the water.'

She got up unsteadily and headed for the stairs, wishing she had more composure, wishing she did not feel as uncomfortable and clumsy as a teenager, wishing he did not have this awful ability to make her feel so . . . so vulnerable.

Upstairs, the bedroom fire burned brightly. Val had stocked the basket with plenty of logs and the room was comfortably warm. Unlike the bathroom, which was freezing, and Sorrel didn't linger in it for very long, despite the hot water.

Tonight she wasn't sleeping in her underwear, but in the nightshirt she had brought with her.

The bed felt surprisingly cold, and she wished she had had the forethought to bring a hot-water bottle with her. Her body slid into the soft dip in the middle and her skin burned suddenly. She couldn't hear a sound from downstairs. She had left the quilt neatly folded outside the bathroom door with one of the pillows. It was true that the bed wasn't anything like as warm without it, but needs must, she told herself.

She closed her eyes and willed herself to go to sleep, but it was impossible. Consequently she was wide awake and tense when the bedroom door opened half an hour later and Val walked in, wearing his towelling robe and carrying both quilt and pillow.

She sat up in bed as he spread the quilt on the bed, and demanded freezingly, 'Just what do you think you're doing?'

'Getting into bed,' he told her affectionately, putting down his pillows and starting to unfasten his robe. 'Move over, otherwise I might be tempted to think you want to spend another night in my arms.'

'We agreed that you were going to sleep downstairs,' Sorrel reminded him, fast losing her temper.

'No, we didn't,' he told her cheerfully. 'You *assumed* my agreement. I never gave it.' He looked thoughtfully at her. 'This is the nineteen eighties,

Sorrel, and personally I can't see a damn thing wrong in a man and a woman sharing the same bed, particularly when not doing so means that one of them is going to have to sleep on a hard stone floor, *particularly* when that one of them is me.'

'All right, then,' Sorrel told him dangerously, 'if *you* won't sleep downstairs, then I will.' She got out of bed, shaking with anger and something else she didn't want to name. Her nightshirt only came midway down her thighs, and she was shivering with cold and emotion as she yanked the quilt off the bed.

'Now, hold on a minute—' Val's hand covered hers.

He'd been wrong about the Victorian nightdress, he reflected, eyeing the slim length of her legs appreciatively. She looked about eighteen, standing there glowering at him, her temper not quite hiding her fear. He felt a momentary pang of remorse and then quelled it. What he was doing was for her own good. Besides, if he let her marry this Andrew . . .

'Let go of the quilt,' Sorrel gritted at him.

'It's mine,' he told her innocently. 'You gave it to me.'

'That was when I thought you were sleeping downstairs. Now *I'm* sleeping there, *I* want the quilt.'

'There's no need,' he told her, adding outrageously, 'Look, if you think I'm worried that you might try to take advantage of me...'

Sorrel stared at him, forgetting to hold on to the quilt in her fury.

'*Me* take advantage of *you*?'

'Well, you're the one who's in a committed relationship,' he told her virtuously. 'You might mistake me for Andrew.'

It was too much. Mistake *him* for Andrew? Never in a thousand years.

'I've already told you,' she stormed at him, 'Andrew and I are not...do not sleep together.'

'Mm...he doesn't know what he's missing,' he told her.

It was several seconds before Sorrel could recover from her rage, but when she did she gave the quilt a vicious tug and then somehow found that, since Val was refusing to let go of it, she was inexorably being pulled onto the bed.

So he thought he could use his superior strength to dominate her, did he? She gritted her teeth and heaved, and then had the extraordinary sensation of hurtling through the air, before landing in a heap on top of the quilt.

'Are you all right?' Val asked her solicitously, but there was amusement in his eyes, and no wonder, Sorrel thought wretchedly, looking down at the tangle of legs and arms on the quilt and realising with mortification that her nightshirt had ridden up almost to the top of her thighs.

'No, I'm not,' she told him furiously. 'You think this is all a game, don't you? Well, it might be to you but...' To her horror, she could feel the tears filling her eyes. Before Val could see them too, she snatched up the quilt and made a bolt for the door, expecting with every step to hear him coming after her.

But he didn't, and although she told herself that she was glad, later, lying chilled and uncomfortable on the kitchen floor, her body all too aware of every ridge in the floor and the hardness of the stone, she couldn't help remembering how deliciously comfortable she had been last night. How beautifully warm...how sensuously relaxed. Sensuously? Her nerve-endings quivered and she closed her eyes determinedly, blotting out her traitorous thoughts.

CHAPTER SIX

SORREL gave a tiny yelp of pain as she turned over and bruised her hip on the hard floor. She felt as though every single bone in her body ached, and she was sure she was going to be covered in a multitude of bruises. If Val had been a gentleman, there was no way he would have let her sleep downstairs. *Andrew* wouldn't have done so. Her bruises were forgotten as she tried to envisage just exactly what her fiancé would have done. Certainly not suggested that they share the bed. No, Andrew would never have suggested that in a hundred years. Nor would Andrew have teased and tormented her, made her laugh and driven her close to the edge of fury, thrown snowballs at her and made her feel...

Feel what? she questioned sharply, sitting abruptly and groaning as she felt her muscles protest. What on earth was the matter with her, sitting here on the verge of stupidity, mooning about a man who by rights she ought to thoroughly detest? He had walked into her life and was virtually trying to turn it upside-down, telling her that she was mad to even think of marrying Andrew. Telling her

that she was hiding away from reality, telling her
that she would regret it if she did go ahead and
marry Andrew.

All nonsense, of course—and yet, was it? She
drew her legs up and wrapped her arms around
them, lowering her head to her knees and staring
musingly into space.

Be honest with yourself, she thought firmly.
Haven't you felt envious of Simon and Fiona?
Haven't you felt as though there's something very
important missing from your relationship with
Andrew?

She moved restlessly, uneasy with the direction
her thoughts were taking, blaming Val for the sudden doubts which seemed to have sprung up in her
mind like a planting of dragon's teeth, even while
she knew that the doubts had already been there
before Val's arrival.

She got up and walked over to the window,
looking out. No sign of a thaw. The sky looked dull
and heavy, laden with the promise of more snow.
She shivered, cold in her nightshirt, trying not to
think of how she had woken up yesterday morning, deliciously warm, her body languorously relaxed, almost as though...

As though what? As though she and Val *had*
made love? An odd sensation vibrated through her
body, an awareness of a need she didn't want to
acknowledge. She was missing Andrew. Once she

was back at home and life had returned to normal, she would forget all these foolish sensations and longings.

But first she would have to share another night alone here at the cottage with Val. Well, this time it would be his turn to sleep on the floor.

There was little point in trying to go back to sleep, so she filled the kettle instead, and went upstairs to get washed and dressed while she waited for it to boil.

There was no sound from the bedroom. Presumably Val was still fast asleep. Well, he would be, wouldn't he? she thought bitterly. He had the bed.

By the time she had made the tea, the faint ache in her skull had turned into a full-blown headache. Tension, she acknowledged tiredly, massaging her scalp. And of course she had not thought to bring any pain-killers with her.

She was sitting in front of the fire, nursing a mug of tea and her grievances, when Val walked into the kitchen.

'Any chance of a second cup of that in the pot?' he asked her cheerfully.

'No,' she told him shortly. 'I just made enough for myself.'

He looked at her for a moment—a thoughtful, concerned look, very different from the way he normally looked at her—and Sorrel had the distinct impression that he was looking right into her

heart and seeing all the panic and fear that was fes-
tering there. She held her breath tensely, waiting for
him to make some comment, to taunt her with his
knowledge of the doubts she was sure must be
written plain there for him to read, but instead he
said wryly, 'My goodness, you are in a bad mood,
aren't you?'

'So would you be if you'd spent the night sleeping on this floor,' Sorrel snapped, relieved and yet
at the same time somehow disappointed that he
hadn't confirmed her fears. Surely she didn't want
him to accuse her of having doubts about the wisdom of her marriage? And yet, if not, why was she
feeling so... almost let down because he had not
said anything?

'Serves you right for being such an idiot,' he told
her unfeelingly. 'Far too stubborn for your own
good, that's what you are.'

Was she? She put her mug down and rubbed her
temple tiredly, trying to ease the pounding ache that
throbbed there.

'Something wrong?'

He was so quick, too quick.

'Headache,' she told him curtly, and looked up
to see that he was frowning with concern. 'It's
nothing,' she assured him, not really knowing why
she wanted to. 'It's just a tension headache. I get
them from time to time.'

'You know what causes those, don't you?' he warned her mockingly.

It was too much. She lost her temper and snapped, 'Yes—tension.'

He was laughing at her, damn him. And she wanted to lash out at him and hurt him the way he was hurting her. Hurting her? She took a deep breath, her eyes betraying her bewilderment.

'Tension is just a word to describe the effect of the suppressing of emotional reactions,' he informed her. 'Reactions such as anger, pain, need...'

Sorrel stiffened weakly. What was he trying to say? She searched his face, looking for some sign that he was baiting her, teasing her, but there was none.

He was telling her that her headache was caused by her own feelings, feelings which she had deliberately repressed, but that wasn't true. It couldn't be true, and she was going to tell him as much.

'If I *am* suppressing anything, it's the anger that *you're* making me feel,' she told him bitterly.

He looked at her for a long time, and it was impossible to drag her gaze away. She felt herself go hot under it, her eyes wide and her emotions all too visible.

'*Is* it only anger, Sorrel?' he asked her quietly.

The kitchen went oddly silent. Sorrel had a momentary feeling of quiet calm and strength, a feeling of some tremendous long-awaited happiness, just within the reach of her fingertips, if only she could stretch out and grasp it. And then the feeling went and in its place came a surge of panic. Of course it was only panic, what else could it be? Was he trying to imply...?

She tilted her chin and looked squarely at him. 'Of course it's only anger.'

'You say it so resolutely. Almost as though you're afraid.'

'Afraid? What is there to be afraid of?'

'This, perhaps,' Val told her almost musingly, almost as though it wasn't serious at all, but just a game—which, of course, it was to him, but not to her. Never to her, she acknowledged achingly as he reached for her and took her in his arms, her body quiescent and waiting, almost as though obeying some alien command which her mind could not hear. The sensation of his arms closing round her was so familiar, so right. She closed her eyes, swaying towards him, and heard him smother a rough sound of pleasure in his throat. It made her tingle all over and open her eyes again. His were so dark, they looked black. They mesmerised her, held her.

'Sorrel.' He said it so quietly, his voice little more than a whisper, tasting her name, tasting *her* in some indefinable way, and then his arms tightened around her and one hand lifted, his fingers sliding through her hair.

'Such a beautiful colour... it feels like silk.' He drew his fingers through it, and then lifted some of the silky strands to his mouth.

His eyes glittered wildly, and she had a momentary vision of herself lying naked in his arms while his mouth caressed her skin through the veil of her hair. It was so erotic that it made her tremble.

'Yes,' she heard him whisper, and then more fiercely, 'Yes. Admit it, Sorrel. You...'

Admit what? Her head spun, the enormity of what she was doing crashing down on her. She tore out of his grasp and, without thinking properly about what she was doing, raced for the back door, opening it and running out into the snow. She heard Val calling her name behind her. Not in a whisper this time, but in a shout that echoed against the snow-covered hills.

She ran from him without knowing why, following an instinct that urged her to flee, even though she had no known goal. He caught up with her as she plunged into the first drift, gasping with shock at the sudden sensation of falling.

As he tried to grab hold of her, Sorrel cried out, terrified by the sudden sensation of plunging down into the deep drift.

Snow engulfed her, drowning her, entombing her, and she did the one thing that all her knowledge and experience should have prepared her against. She panicked.

She tried to draw deep gulps of air into her lungs, and then choked as her mouth filled with snow. It was everywhere, pressing on her, menacing her, obliterating her ability to see and hear. She struggled to free herself of its smothering weight.

Where was Val? Was he going to punish her by letting her suffocate and die?

She tried to cry out, but she couldn't breathe. To even try to do so hurt her lungs. She felt curiously dizzy and warm, which was silly when she was buried in freezing snow, and perhaps if she didn't try to breathe that awful pain would go away.

'Sorrel.'

She heard the frantic voice and its urgency, but it was too much of an effort to respond to it—and then she was brutally wrenched from her cocooning prison, and someone was holding her. She tried to open her eyes, but the light was too bright; the cold air stung her skin. She felt hands on her chest, moving in a businesslike fashion, and then a warm, vital mouth breathing life into her.

Val was giving her the kiss of life, she realised, suddenly snapping back to life, and squirming away from him.

'Sorrel, are you all right?'

She opened her eyes and looked at him, shocked by the colour of his skin. Beneath his tan he looked haggard—and no wonder... She tried to imagine how he would have broken the news to her parents, and then realised with a horribly weakening surge of shock how easily a tragedy could have happened. And it would have been her own fault. She knew how deeply the snow drifted here, within yards of safety and the farmhouse, through an act of almost criminal stupidity. She wouldn't have blamed Val if he had taken hold of her and shaken her, but instead he was touching her almost tenderly as he helped her to her feet, gently encouraging her to walk, and then abruptly changing his mind and swinging her up into his arms.

As he carried her towards the farmhouse, she discovered that she was shaking, or was it Val? She must have frightened the life out of him. He must have lightning-quick reactions to have realised her danger, and dug through the snow to find her.

She expected him to put her down in the kitchen, but he didn't. He carried her upstairs to the bedroom, where the fire still glowed and the air was so warm that her body was attacked by pins and needles driving out the freezing chill of the snow.

He put her down in front of the fire as carefully as though she was made of spun glass.

'Don't you dare move,' he warned her rawly. And then he was gone, leaving her to shiver and wonder weakly if she was ever going to be able to move again. Now that the danger had passed, reaction was beginning to set in. She started to shiver and tremble, her teeth chattering audibly.

She plucked at her snow-caked clothes with half-numb fingers that trembled far too much to allow her to deal with the necessary zips and buttons, and suddenly Val was back, oddly grim-faced, and looking dizzyingly male, despite the fact that he was carrying a couple of large pink bathsheets.

He kneeled down beside her, putting them down. Then, holding her gently, he proceeded to undress her, far more deftly and capably than she could have done, all the time keeping up a calming flow of conversation, talking to her in the same kind of gentle voice he might have used to a terrified child, she recognised inwardly, while she protested and complained crossly that he was not to touch her and that she could manage for herself, even though she knew that she could not.

And then it was too late. He had stripped her down to her bra and briefs, and when he discovered that they too were wet he removed those as well; but there was no time for her to feel embarrassed or vulnerable, because his attention wasn't on her nude body, with its fine Celtic skin and soft womanly curves, but on the bathsheet in which he was engulfing her, rubbing the fabric hard against her skin.

She yelped sharply in protest, trying to wriggle away as the blood flooded back into her numbed extremities and sent piercing attacks of pins and needles burning through them.

Within seconds she was glowing with warmth, her shivers ceasing and her body coming vigorously back to life.

'How do you feel?' Val asked her tersely, sitting back on his heels and studying her flushed face with its halo of hair.

'Foolish,' she told him frankly. 'That was an idiotic thing to do...running out like that. If you hadn't been there...'

'If I hadn't been there, it wouldn't have happened in the first place,' he told her grimly. 'Don't take all the blame on your own shoulders. I'm sorry if what I said about your engagement upset you.'

'It wasn't that.' He looked so tired and drawn. She wanted to reach out and touch him, to stroke the soft hair that lay at the nape of his neck, to cradle his head against her breast and reassure him that she was all right.

He looked at her, the tiredness falling away, his expression suddenly alert, and then his gaze dropped to her mouth and lingered there.

Her heart seemed to jump frantically and the heat that washed her had nothing to do with the warmth of the room.

'Oh, Sorrel,' he groaned, reaching for her, framing her face with hands that trembled. 'Heaven forgive me, I shouldn't be doing this.'

His mouth touched hers, his lips warm and firm, trembling slightly in a way that was gut-wrenchingly exciting as she felt his emotion and yielded herself to it in a mindless act of need.

Later she was to wonder if he had only meant the kiss to be a brief caress…if it was her own blind yielding that fuelled the passion that erupted between them, burning white-hot and out of control, as he bit fiercely at her mouth, his fingers hard against her skin, his body arching hers back, the towel bunched up between them. Her lips parted, soft and moist and swollen into a sensitivity that made her tremble wildly as his tongue touched her lips.

Against her mouth he muttered hoarsely, 'So sensitive. Oh, you'd go crazy in my arms if I did that to you here.''

His hand touched her breast through the thickness of the towel, and she shook as much at what he had said as at what he had done. As though to confirm his words, her breasts swelled and ached tormentingly.

'I've got to feel you against me. Just this once.'

And before she could stop him he was pushing away the towel, and pressing her against his body. She felt the roughness of his jeans against her thighs and the hardness of the body inside them. His belt buckle dug into her skin and she tried to squirm away.

'What's wrong?'

She had never seen a man's eyes darken with such passion, the heat of it reflected in the long burn of colour on his cheekbones. A muscle pulsed quickly in his throat.

She swallowed hard, feeling her own blood pick up the giddy rhythm of his. 'Your belt. It hurts...' She spoke slowly, as though language was an unfamiliar means of communication.

'Where...where does it hurt you?' he demanded rawly, and the sensation of his hand suddenly covering her stomach made her cry out sharply and ache to push herself against him.

He had gone very still, and she saw that he was looking at her breasts. Her skin was so white compared with his, white and blue-veined, her nipples flushed and swollen. She saw the breath he drew lift his chest and felt his tension. He reached out and touched her, cupping her gently, as though he found her body an awesome mystery.

'Shall I show you how I can make you feel?' he asked her, and the words seemed to echo round the room. She closed her eyes and imagined how it would feel to have his mouth against her flesh. 'Don't marry him, Sorrel.'

She flinched as his words broke the spell, and made to pull away from him. She saw the passion die out of his eyes, to be replaced by a gentler emotion. His hands came up to cup her face, holding it gently. She could have moved away, but she didn't.

'It's all right,' he told her softly. 'There's no need to be scared. What happened was a moment out of time…something born out of my fear that…' He broke off, his hands gentle as they moulded her face. He bent his head and placed a healing, passionless kiss against her mouth. 'I'm sorry. Will you forgive me?'

Tears stung her eyes. What was there to forgive? She was equally to blame, and she clung to the excuse he had offered her like the survivor of a sunken ship to a piece of wreckage. Of course he was right. That passion, that need—hers as well as his—had been born out of the intense emotion of their fear. It had been a natural reaction. And, now the danger was past, life was back to normal. Here was her second cousin however many times removed from Australia, and she was Andrew's fiancé.

'It's OK,' she told him shakily. 'I think we both over-reacted.' She offered him a tremulous smile, and then tensed as she saw his eyes darken as though…as though…

'Come on,' he said gruffly, picking her up. 'Let's get you tucked up properly in bed.'

'In bed? I'm not an invalid,' she protested. 'I'm perfectly capable of getting dressed and coming downstairs.'

She saw that he looked dubious, and felt a wave of tenderness wash over her. She was so used to being thought of as practical and independent that it came as a shock to recognise how much she liked the thought of leaning on him, even if only briefly.

'Are you sure you'll be all right?' he asked her, touching her shoulder briefly.

She nodded, turning her face away so that he wouldn't see how much that touch pleased her.

'Leave the door open,' he told her as he walked toward it. 'Just in case you do need me.'

SHE DIDN'T. She managed to change into clean dry clothes and get herself back downstairs, and she told herself that the trembly sensation in the pit of her stomach when she walked into the kitchen and looked at him came from a purely physical weakness caused by the accident.

'Come and sit down,' he urged her. He was looking at her as though he half expected her to disappear in front of him. She must have given him a terrible fright. She reached out and touched his wrist.

Beneath her fingertips, she could feel the crispness of his dark body hair. It sent an electric tingle jolting down her arm. He moved away abruptly, almost as though he didn't want her to touch him, she recognised.

'Your prophecy yesterday about them finding us frozen in the snow wasn't so far out, after all,' she joked, trying to lighten the tension. To her shock, his face drained of colour and he looked at her with haunted, bitter eyes.

'For Pete's sake,' he demanded thickly, 'what are you trying to do to me?'

'It was a joke, Val. I...' She saw that the hand he rubbed over his face was shaking slightly. Of course he would be shaken. He would be feeling responsible. He was that kind of man...allowing himself now that the danger was over to imagine what it would have been like facing her family, telling them... She gave a small shudder and begged huskily, 'Look, let's just forget about the whole thing. It was my fault for behaving so stupidly. If you hadn't been here...'

'If I hadn't been here, it would never have happened in the first place. The sooner either the thaw comes or your brother arrives, the happier I'm going to be.'

Sentiments she thoroughly echoed. Didn't she? Sorrel asked herself as she watched him pouring them both large mugs of coffee.

'Here, drink this,' he told her gruffly. 'I reckon we both need the kick of the caffeine. About what happened upstairs—' he added, but Sorrel didn't want to hear whatever it was he was going to say. She wanted to forget the entire incident had ever taken place. Forget that she had ever...ever felt that need to be a part of him, that desire...that intensity of pleasure.

'Val, please, let's just forget it. Please,' she begged.

He looked at her for a long time and then asked her tautly, 'Will you tell Andrew about it?'

Her heart thumped against her ribs. Would she? She cleared her throat and looked away from him.

'I don't know,' she told him honestly. There was enough pain and uncertainty in her voice for him to hear them and curse himself again for what he had done. He should never have touched her, never have kissed her, never have... But it was too late. Looking at her, he wondered cynically if his desire to separate her from her fiancé had ever been entirely altruistic. Well, his sisters would have a laugh at his expense if they ever found out. He tried to imagine himself years from this moment, looking back at it and not feeling any pain, but he couldn't. How ironic life could be...

IT WAS GONE midnight, and as yet Val had made no effort to suggest that either of them went to bed. She couldn't face another night on the kitchen floor; her body ached in a thousand places as it was.

She gave him a surreptitious glance beneath her lashes. She had seldom seen a more male man; every movement he made was loaded with animal grace.

She stifled a large yawn, but not before he had caught the small betraying sound. He put down the diary he was studying and asked curtly, 'Tired?'

She nodded. He got up and walked over to the window. The day had been cold, with flurries of snow.

'Wind's changed,' he told her.

She got up and joined him, listening as he had done. 'Maybe that will mean a thaw.'

'Let's hope so,' he told her grimly, and then he turned to her and told her bleakly, 'You're quite safe with me, Sorrel. If you're putting off going to bed because you're afraid—'

'No,' she checked him quickly.

'I'm not sleeping on the floor,' he told her, 'and neither are you. We both need a good night's sleep, Sorrel,' he added in a more gentle tone. 'I promise you you've nothing to fear. I won't touch you.'

'Nor pretend that I touched you?' she asked him wryly, her heart lifting when she saw a trace of a smile warm his eyes. It was disconcerting how much she had missed the teasing looks he gave her, the light in his eyes when they warmed with laughter.

'Nor pretend that you touched me,' he agreed.

'I'll go up then,' she suggested, since there seemed nothing else to say. He was right, she *was* exhausted; shock had taken its toll on her and it must have done on him as well. She must not forget that for him the shock had probably been

greater, because he had known that the full responsibility for getting her out of the drift alive lay
with him.

She tried to imagine Andrew coping with such a
situation, but couldn't. Andrew would have panicked and fussed. Andrew wouldn't have had the
first idea what to do. Andrew would have let her
die, she acknowledged bleakly.

CHAPTER SEVEN

DURING the night the weather changed with an abrupt turn-about carried on a warm westerly wind, but neither of the occupants of the comfortable double bed were aware of it.

The noise of the wind did make Sorrel stir briefly, but only to snuggle more closely into the curve of Val's body as he obligingly accommodated her persistent burrowing movements and curled a proprietory arm around her in his sleep.

Strain and exhaustion had taken their toll on both of them, and neither of them heard the Land Rover rattle into the farmyard over the melting snow and ice.

Simon had left Ludlow early, as anxious as the rest of the family to find out if the two girls were all right.

He sounded the Land Rover horn before getting out, and Val heard it, waking instantly, to give Sorrel a warning shake.

She was still curled up next to him, and as he looked down into her face he reflected that he had never seen such perfect skin. He reached out and touched her cheek gently with his fingertips, unable to resist the impulse. Her eyelashes fluttered and her eyes opened.

'There's someone outside,' he told her.

For a moment it didn't penetrate, and then Sorrel shot up in bed, demanding, 'What?'

They both heard the tread of feet on the stairs at the same time, the sound accompanied by off-key whistling.

'Simon,' Sorrel groaned, recognising her brother's familiar whistle. 'Oh, no... It must have thawed.' She made to leap out of the bed, but Val restrained her, shaking his head when he saw the panic in her eyes.

'We haven't done anything wrong,' he reminded her quietly. 'There's no need to be afraid.'

And then Simon rapped briefly on the door and pushed it open.

'Sorrel, are you awake?' he began, only to stare at the bed and its two occupants in mute disbelief.

'Good lord, Sorrel!' he exclaimed. 'What...'

His attention swung from his sister to her companion as Val pushed aside the bedclothes and reached for his jeans.

'This is Cousin Val,' Sorrel said weakly, and then, before her brother could ask her any questions, picked up her own clothes and fled to the bathroom, cravenly leaving it to Val to make the necessary explanations.

She stayed there until Val came and knocked on the door and told her, 'Coffee's ready, Sorrel, and your brother wants to make an early start back.'

Reluctantly she opened the door.

'What did Simon say?' she whispered frantically.

Why on earth had they had to oversleep this morning, of all mornings? What on earth must Simon be thinking? What on earth had Val told him? It had been idiotic of her to run away like that. Heaven knew what tales Val had been telling Simon. Her brother would have understood, if she'd explained what had happened properly, but now...

'He says he wants to start back as soon as possible,' Val told her cheerfully.

'No, not about that. I meant about...'

'Finding us in bed together?' Val asked her drily, laughing a little unkindly at her expression. 'Poor Sorrel, but you're so easy to tease.'

There was no hint of passion in his eyes, no awareness of her as a woman, no trace of yesterday's tenderness; they were back to their old footing, which was what she wanted, and yet...

Val saw the expressions chase one another across her face and hid his own feelings. It had been very enlightening, talking to her brother. He had discovered from Simon that the rest of her family shared his own views about her engagement, and once he had explained the situation, confided in Simon that...

'Your coffee will be getting cold,' he reminded her, 'and I still have to get washed and dressed.'

Sorrel went downstairs slowly, hesitating just outside the kitchen, and then, taking a deep breath, she pushed open the door, reminding herself that she had done nothing wrong. There was nothing for her to be ashamed of.

'Oh, there you are,' Simon commented, pushing a mug of coffee towards her. 'Ma's been going frantic about the pair of you up here. She'll be relieved when she discovers that you had Val to take care of you.'

'I don't need anyone to take care of me. I'm an adult, not a child,' Sorrel countered, and then bit her lip. 'You must have got quite a surprise when you discovered...that is, when you realised that Val was a man.'

'Not as much a shock as you evidently got,' Simon told her, chuckling appreciatively, and a little of her apprehension died away. Whatever Val had said to Simon had obviously had the effect of reassuring her brother as to the innocence of their behaviour.

She picked up her coffee, clasping the mug in both hands, and said huskily 'Simon, you won't say anything about...about this morning, will you?'

'By *anyone,* I presume you mean Andrew,' he asked her drily. 'You've no fears there, Sorrel. Your fiancé and I don't exactly go in for intimate heart-to-heart chats.' He saw her face and walked over to her, hugging her. 'Look, sis, it's all right. Val's explained everything to me, and I promise that I won't say a word to Andrew. I wouldn't have said anything anyway, you know,' he added wryly. 'You are an adult, as you've just pointed out, and whatever you choose to do in your private life . . .'

'Simon, that's just the point. It wasn't like that—' she began, but Simon wasn't listening to her.

He had gone over to the window to look outside, and said to her over his shoulder, 'I'm not sure how long the thaw's going to last, but I don't want to hang around up here. How quickly can you be packed and ready to leave?'

DESPITE SIMON'S assurances, all the way home Sorrel worried that he wouldn't be able to resist the opportunity to tease her by revealing the compromising position in which he had found them. Her family would understand, of course, but she knew how much they all disapproved of her engagement. If Simon should take it into his head to say something to Andrew . . . The wisest course would be for her to tell Andrew what had happened herself. There was, after all, no real reason why he shouldn't know...was there?

She had elected to sit in the rear of the Land Rover, insisting that Val take the front passenger seat next to Simon. She was deep in thought, and he made her jump when he suddenly turned round and said quietly to her, 'For Pete's sake, Sorrel, what kind of man is he? If he loves you...'

'He does,' she told him hurriedly, 'and besides,' she fibbed, 'I wasn't thinking about Andrew.'

'Liar,' he mocked her softly. 'You're worrying yourself sick about what's going to happen if he finds out.'

'No. No, I'm not.'

'We'll be in Ludlow in ten minutes,' Simon called over his shoulder above the noise of the engine. 'Warn Val to look out for the castle, Sorrel.'

Dutifully she pointed it out to him, wishing she didn't feel quite so acutely conscious of him as he turned round in his seat, leaning one arm along it as he looked in the direction she was pointing.

She had to sit on the edge of her own seat in order to make herself heard above the noise of the engine, and consequently, when Simon had to brake suddenly, she shot forward and would have ended up on the floor if Val hadn't reacted with lightning speed and caught hold of her.

The sensation of his hands holding her and his warm breath on her skin instantly transported her back to the moment when he had kissed her with such fierce passion.

She went white at the unexpectedness of the piercingly sweet sensation the memory brought, causing Val to hold her even tighter and demand urgently, 'Sorrel, what is it? Are you all right?'

At first she thought he was mocking her, that he knew quite well what was wrong with her, and then she saw the anxiety in his eyes and guilt replaced her pain.

'I'm fine,' she told him shakily, but she knew it wasn't true and that she was far from fine, that she would never be 'fine' again.

He had come into her life and completely torn apart all her carefully erected plans for the way she wanted to live her life, and now she was floundering in a morass of self-doubts and fears, with no clear point to aim for.

'Soon be home,' Simon told them, adding warningly, 'Ma's got the red carpet out...to make up to you for having to shunt off to the farm with only Sorrel for company.' He grinned across at Val. 'Boy, is she going to get a shock when she sees you!'

'Not too much of a shock, I trust,' Val returned evenly, and although the words were calm and bland Sorrel felt as though he was giving Simon a firm warning.

About what? About not revealing the compromising situation in which he had found them? An unfamiliar sense of warmth enveloped her...a feeling of being protected and cherished, a feeling of security in knowing that Val stood between her and the questions that were bound to come.

Of course he's not doing it to protect you, she derided herself inwardly. He's doing it for his own protection. He doesn't want the whole family coming down on him—with questions, and then her stomach muscles tensed as the farm came in view. Simon was busy pointing out to Val the boundaries to their land, and explaining how they farmed. They turned into the yard and her mother came bustling out, her face pink with excitement.

'Ma, have I got a surprise for you,' Simon called out to her as he stopped the Land Rover. 'Come and meet Cousin Val.'

Sorrel watched the shock register on her mother's face and saw the searching, worried look she gave him as Val stepped out of the Land Rover and shook hands with her.

'It seems I've caused everyone around here a lot of problems,' Sorrel heard him apologising easily. 'It never occurred to me that you'd think I was a girl. Sorrel's been magnificent about coping with the situation, although I suspect her fiancé might have one or two searching questions to ask me. Unfortunately I'm going to have to admit that I was out of luck and she seems to have the bad taste to prefer him to me,' he added with mock sadness, and then he turned to the Land Rover and held his hand out to her and said, 'Come on down here, Sorrel, and show your mother that you're still all in one piece.'

He had struck just the right touch; the apprehension had lifted from her mother's face and now she was exclaiming that in view of the weather it was probably just as well that Sorrel had had a man with her to take charge.

Her mother would never gain the approval of the feminist lobby, Sorrel recognised wryly, getting out of the Land Rover.

She hadn't anticipated the warm clasp of Val's hand on her own as he drew her towards him, tucking her against his side, and keeping her in a manner so fraternally affectionate that he might indeed have been her brother. That this piece of skilled sideplay was for her mother's benefit, Sorrel was quite sure, a suspicion that was confirmed when he told her jocularly, 'I've warned Sorrel that while I'm over here she's going to have to step into my sisters' shoes and become my sister elect, so to speak.'

'You have sisters?' her mother enquired, diverted.

'Yup. Three of them, to be exact. They boss the life out of me. I've brought photographs with me, but they're in my car.'

There had been no sign of his abandoned car by the side of the road, and Simon had told him that it had most probably been towed away to the nearest garage. He had offered to check with the police as to its whereabouts once they were home, and all this was explained to the family as Val was hustled inside.

Only Sorrel hung back, feeling oddly as though she had just lost something. Val was still holding her hand, and he tugged on it.

'What's wrong, Sorrel? Aren't you coming inside?' her mother questioned.

'I expect she wants to be on her own to telephone that fiancé of hers. I'm sure he's been burning the telephone lines between here and his home, worrying about how she's been getting on,' Val added with gentle malice. 'I sure wouldn't like to think of any fiancée of mine being snowed in, at some remote farm.'

He was pushing her, prompting her, and there was nothing she could do but swallow down her ire and say brightly, 'He's probably been away at one of his book fairs most of the time. Andrew buys and sells old books,' she added for Val's benefit. 'He spends a lot of time away.'

'Does he?' Val murmured, looking suitably surprised. He turned to her mother. 'Well, now, if I had a fiancée as beautiful as Sorrel, I don't think I'd be too happy with that kind of situation.'

Sorrel gritted her teeth as her mother rewarded him with an approving smile.

'That's just what I keep telling Sorrel,' she beamed at him. 'I keep saying to her, "Sorrel dear, he's such a laggard lover, are you sure that...?"'

'Mother,' Sorrel interrupted grimly. 'I'm sure Val doesn't want to hear all about that.'

'Oh, I do,' Val corrected her innocently. 'I'm interested in everything about my new family. Do you know,' he added thoughtfully to Sorrel's mother as she led him inside, 'we have a photograph of one of my great-aunts at home, and I could swear there is a likeness between her and Sorrel.'

Behind him, Sorrel grinned to herself, and then murmured softly to him, 'If that's true, it's a miracle. I take after my mother's side of the family, not my father's.'

The look he gave her was completely unrepentant, and she ought to be grateful to him, Sorrel acknowledged fair-mindedly, because he had certainly won her mother over and very skilfully averted any crises about the propriety of them spending the last three days together. Her mother was as relaxed and comfortable with him as though she had known him all his life, whereas with Andrew, whom she *had* in fact known since he was a schoolboy, she was frequently ill at ease.

Andrew did not fit in with her family. He allowed them to see how contemptuous he was of what he termed their 'bucolic pursuits'. He had no interest in farming, nor pretended to have any. He hated the dirt and the mud, and he visited the farm as infrequently as he could, always finding some excuse to avoid the invitations her mother gave him to join in their family celebrations.

Lunch during the week was normally a snatched affair, work on the farm not allowing for more than a brief break during the day, and in the mêlée of people coming and going, lambs bleating for their food, dogs barking and her father complaining that he was damned if he was going to fill in any more Ministry forms, Sorrel managed somehow to answer the family's questions without betraying too much of what had actually happened.

'Yes,' she admitted, 'it *was* a shock to find that Cousin Val was a man and not a woman...'

'But it must have been a relief to you as well, dear,' her mother put in solicitously, 'especially as Val arrived in the middle of the snowstorm. You must have been worried about being snowed up in there on your own. V—'

'Relieved doesn't cover it, does it, Sorrel?' Simon teased her wickedly, having heard all about her initial reaction to him from Val.

Giving her brother an indignant look, Sorrel reflected that Simon and Val seemed to have become firm friends already, and now Fiona, looking prettily flushed and blooming with the knowledge of her pregnancy, was plying him with questions, and receiving from him the kind of teasingly flirtatious answers that made her laugh and shake a warning finger at him, telling him that she was not fooled by his demeanour.

While their mother's back was turned, Simon whispered just loudly enough for Sorrel to hear, to his wife, 'It seems that we've got a treat in store when we do move in up there. Gran and Gramps' old bed is so comfortable that...'

Sorrel went bright red and hissed furiously at him, 'Simon, you dare...' And when their mother turned round he was eyeing her with mock virtuous bewilderment, asking her exactly what she meant.

'Nothing,' she muttered bitterly.

Amy Llewellyn, who was by no means as naïve as her family sometimes liked to think, looked thoughtfully at her daughter's flushed face, but wisely said nothing.

When lunch was finished, she suggested kindly to Sorrel, 'Darling, you must be worn out, but I'm afraid there were several business calls for you while you were away. I've made a list of them and left it in your workroom.'

'I'll go and check through them,' Sorrel announced, thankful to have a legitimate opportunity of escaping.

'I'd like to see where you work,' Val announced, standing up and saying to her mother, 'I was fascinated, watching Sorrel work on her tapestry, and I was hoping I might be able to persuade her to design one of her rugs for me to take home with me.'

'I'm sure she will,' Amy agreed, adding firmly, 'I'll take you up to your room, Val. You'll want to ring the police and track down your car. If they've taken it to the local garage, Dai Jones who runs it knows us well, and we'll be able to make some arrangement to get it here for you.' Val, far shrewder and more aware than Sorrel, knew when he had been out-manoeuvred and gave way with a good grace.

'So, tell me a little more about your family,' Amy Llewellyn commanded as she led Val away to his room.

He obliged her.

As she opened the door to his room, Amy added, 'And you and Sorrel managed all right at the farmhouse?'

'Managed very well,' he agreed blandly, and then closed the bedroom door and walked over to the window which looked down on to the stableyard. Amy followed him, wondering what had caught his attention. Sorrel was standing there, bareheaded, the wind teasing her bright hair, her head thrown back in a familiar gesture of defiance as she argued with her brother.

'She's a very special person,' Val murmured, and then, looking directly at Amy, added quietly, 'Far too special to throw herself away on this idiot she's got herself engaged to.'

It was a good fifteen minutes before Amy emerged from Val's room, her face slightly pink with excitement and pleasure. She had liked him from the start, she told herself as she went downstairs.

THE PHONE CALL came right in the middle of the evening meal, a time sacrosanct to the serious business of eating, and Sorrel saw her father frown as he pushed his chair back and got up to answer the phone.

His frown deepened abruptly, and then he held the receiver out to Sorrel. 'It's for you.'

Sorrel picked up the receiver reluctantly. She could tell from her father's expression that it was Andrew who was on the phone, and she had no real wish to speak to him with the rest of her family listening. They appeared to have taken Val to their collective bosom in a way that they had never welcomed Andrew.

'Darling, I just thought I'd give you a ring to let you know I'm back. Mother has invited us over for dinner on Sunday and I've accepted. I'm afraid I can't pick you up because she's asked me if I'll drive over and get Jane—'

'Jane?' Sorrel questioned, even though she knew who he meant.

'Yes, darling. Jane Usher... mother's goddaughter. You have met her.'

'Oh, yes,' Sorrel agreed grimly. Jane Usher was a great favourite of Andrew's mother. She made no bones about the fact that in her estimation Jane would have been the perfect daughter-in-law, and Sorrel had to suppress her irritation with Andrew, who seemed blind to his mother's very obvious machinations to bring the two of them together.

She thought of how little she was likely to enjoy Sunday lunch spent in the company of her mother-in-law-to-be and Jane, and ground her teeth silently, a sudden spurt of rebellion making her say tentatively, 'Andrew, I'm not sure if I can make it on Sunday. We have a visitor. Look, can we discuss it tomorrow evening?' she asked him, suddenly conscious of the silence from the dinner-table. She didn't want to have to start making awkward explanations as to how Valerie had turned out to be Valentine with her entire family listening in.

She and Andrew always had a drink and then a meal together on Friday evenings at the Stag, a local pub-cum-restaurant, but to her chagrin Andrew announced casually, ''Fraid I'm going to have to cancel tomorrow, darling. Jane was telling me about the father of a friend of hers. It appears that he has the most fabulous library, and she's arranged for us to go and meet him tomorrow evening. I'm picking her up after I close the shop. Look, I'm sure your cousin won't mind about Sunday. Can you be at mother's for one o'clock sharp? You know how she feels about punctuality.' A reference to the one occasion on which she had been five minutes late because of a bad traffic jam outside Ludlow.

Sorrel fought back the many acid comments souring her tongue, and held her peace. She was not going to be able to say what she wanted to say to Andrew with an audience. She was furious that he had so thoughtlessly ignored the fact that they normally went out on Fridays simply because he wanted to go and look at someone's library. A visit artfully arranged by 'dear, sweet Jane' to coincide with the one night of the week when they always went out together. Chance? Somehow Sorrel did not think so.

'Is Andrew all right, dear?' her mother enquired solicitously when she went back to the table. Her food had gone cold and she had been hungry, but now her appetite had vanished and she pushed her plate aside.

'Yes,' she said tersely.

'He must have been concerned when he realised you were snowed in,' Val commented watching her.

'Oh, he doesn't know yet, does he, Sorrel?' Fiona interrupted innocently. 'He didn't ring at all while you were up at the farm.'

Sorrel flushed angrily. She knew that Fiona had spoken in genuine innocence, but the look in Val's eyes made her miserably aware of Andrew's short-comings as a concerned lover. He was more emotionally attached to his books than he was to her, she decided wrathfully, and then got angry with herself because she had known that their emotional attachment was tepid all along, and that had been what she wanted.

'Well, never mind, you'll be seeing him tomorrow evening as usual,' her mother put in soothingly.

Sorrel, conscious of everyone's eyes on her, had to admit grimly, 'We're not going out tomorrow. Andrew is going to look at someone's books.'

There was a small silence, and then unexpectedly it was Val who came to her rescue, saying reasonably, 'That's one of the problems of running one's own business, I'm afraid. It does tend to interfere with your private life. Actually, I was hoping to take you all out for a meal while I'm here. Perhaps tomorrow evening would be a good time. The police *had* organised for my hire car to be taken to the local garage, and they've arranged for someone to bring it over here tomorrow, so how about us all going out together?'

'Sounds lovely,' Fiona enthused. 'There's that fabulous new place that's opened. They have a dinner dance on Fridays and—' She broke off and laughed. 'I'm sorry, I . . .'

'Don't apologise,' Val told her with a warm smile. 'I was just going to ask if there was anywhere locally someone could recommend. That sounds ideal.'

'So you won't be seeing Andrew until next week, then?' Simon commented casually, reintroducing him into the conversation when the arrangements for the following evening had been sorted out to everyone's satisfaction.

'What?' Sorrel frowned. 'Oh, no . . . I'm having lunch with him and his mother on Sunday.'

Simon pulled a face. He knew Andrew's mother, since he and Andrew had been at school together.

'Simon, that's enough,' Amy reproved. 'Will Andrew be picking you up, dear?'

'No,' Sorrel told her shortly, and out of the corner of her eyes she saw Val lift his eyebrows. Why on earth were they plaguing her with these embarrassing questions? Normally her family weren't in the least bit interested in her relationship with Andrew, preferring to forget that he existed.

'No? Transport problems?' Val asked sympathetically.

Recklessly, Sorrel looked squarely at him and said coldly, 'No. He's picking up his mother's god-daughter.' She flung down her napkin and pushed back her chair. 'And now, if you've all finished questioning me, I've got some work to do.'

She heard her mother calling her name as she hurried out of the room. It was true she did have work to do, but that wasn't the reason why she had suddenly needed to get away from them. She had just caught the glance of mingled pity and concern that Fiona and Simon had exchanged, and had known with cruel clarity that, in her family's eyes, her relationship with Andrew was being revealed as the poor thing they considered it was. They pitied her, she recognised unhappily. They didn't think that Andrew loved her, that he cared enough about her to put her first. And they were right. But she had always known that, known it and accepted it with the comfortable knowledge that their relationship would hold no dangers for her, that she would never have to fear losing all control and restraint in his arms the way she had seen that woman do.

And yet, now that she had actually had a taste of what it *would* be like to abandon herself to desire, she found she was regretting that she would never know that tingling excitement, that anticipation, that deluge of sensation, and because of *that* she was finding fault with Andrew in a way she had never done before.

She walked into her workroom and stood there, clenching her hands, unwilling to admit the truth. She heard the door open behind her and knew without turning round who had followed her.

She looked at him and said bitterly, 'It's all your fault. *You're* making everything go wrong.' And then to her own acute horror she actually stamped her foot as petulantly as a small child, and completed the débâcle by bursting into tears.

She was still berating him when Val took her into his arms and held her there, rocking her gently, murmuring soothing words of nonsense, telling her that he understood everything and that it would do her good to let go and have a thoroughly good cry.

As she listened to him, the independent, mature side of her nature wanted to protest that his remarks were shockingly sexist and that she ought to pull herself out of his arms and behave like the adult that she was. But the only effect the mangled protest that finally emerged from her lips had was to make Val gather her even more closely against his body, his hand stroking her hair, his lips only a breath away from her ear as he cuddled her and comforted her and told her that since she was, so to speak, 'standing in' for his sisters, it was his brotherly duty to do so, and that not even the most zealous fiancé could find any objections to his behaviour.

The mention of the word 'fiancé' set Sorrel off into another flood of tears, for some reason she wasn't able to define, but it seemed that Val could, because he made some soothing comment about the shocking behaviour of men who put their mother's wishes above those of their fiancée's and who, moreover, were too stupid to see when those same mothers were deliberately manoeuvring them.

'I've had the same trouble myself,' he assured her, making her gulp and stop crying.

'Have you?'

'Mmm...'

Somehow or other Sorrel discovered that Val had led her over to the shabby settee, and that he was now sitting on it with her on his knee.

'Mothers get like that when their sons get past thirty without producing a wife. Mine's been trying to get me married off for years, and she's got more friends with daughters than any woman has a right to have,' he added darkly.

'Is that why you came over here?' Sorrel asked him drily. 'To run away from your mother's machinations?'

'Something like that,' he agreed, but there was a gleam in his eyes which made Sorrel suspect that she had said something which amused him, although she couldn't think what it was.

'Come on,' he told her, pushing her gently off his knee and getting up. 'We'd better get back to the house.'

As she stood up and started to walk away, he checked her and asked quietly, 'Do you love him, Sorrel?'

Immediately Sorrel's mood changed, and she remembered how vulnerable she was to him.

'That's none of your business,' she told him, her head held high.

Behind her, Val muttered something she didn't quite catch, but she knew the words had a derogatory, almost bitter inflection that made her skin burn.

It was all his fault, she told herself angrily. All of it. He had burst into her life and turned it completely upside-down, and she hated him. Hated him.

CHAPTER EIGHT

SORREL hadn't intended going with the others to the dinner dance. She had decided that she would refuse to join them politely but firmly. She would remind them and herself that she was engaged to Andrew and that there were a dozen or more things she could do to fill in her time, which did not include being in Val's company. But on impulse on Friday morning she offered to drive into Ludlow to do her mother's shopping. It would give her the opportunity to pop into the bookshop and acquaint Andrew with the happenings of the last few days, something she was reluctant to do with Jane and his mother as an interested audience. As Sorrel knew from previous experience, once Andrew's mother had her victims firmly in her grasp, she was reluctant to let them go. Sorrel doubted that she and Andrew would be granted so much as five minutes alone on Sunday.

She parked her car on the piece of rough land just outside the town that was used as one of its main car parks, and then set out for the shops.

They were busy, and it took her rather longer than she had anticipated to get everything on her mother's list. On her way to the greengrocers, she passed a dress shop with its window arranged for spring. An evening dress in brilliant blue silk caught her eye and she paused to admire it. It was a colour that particularly suited her; the dress was simplicity itself and stunningly effective. She sighed faintly as she looked at it. No doubt it would be horrendously expensive, and besides, Andrew liked her to wear plain, neat clothes rather like those favoured by his mother, and she had gradually discarded the vivid colours she had worn before their engagement.

It was almost lunchtime before she had all her shopping stowed away in the boot of her car. Andrew's bookshop was in the old part of the town, and she was breathless after the steep climb to reach it.

The shop was empty when she walked in, but she could hear muted voices from the rear stockroom, and without stopping to think she pushed aside the curtain and walked in.

Jane and Andrew were standing close together, poring over the book that Andrew was holding.

Jane saw her first and looked up, her eyes widening and her face colouring uncomfortably.

'Sorrel, what on earth are you doing here?' Andrew exclaimed.

His question was more critical than lover-like, Sorrel recognised as she fought to suppress her own feelings of anger and humiliation to say brightly, 'Oh, Mother asked me to come in and do her shopping, and I thought I'd call round and see if I could coax you out to lunch, if Jane doesn't mind,' she added pointedly.

Instantly Jane flushed vividly and crept closer to Andrew's side... like a little mouse being terrorised by a large cat, Sorrel thought viciously, knowing which role had been cast for *her*. She saw Andrew frown as he looked at her, the frown softening as he smiled at Jane.

'Jane's come over here specially to help me this afternoon so that we can leave early,' he reproved Sorrel. 'I can hardly leave her here on her own. Besides,' he added awkwardly, 'I'd already invited Jane out to lunch. You're welcome to join us...'

As welcome as an outbreak of the Black Death, Sorrel thought bitterly as she gave them both a tight smile and explained that she had changed her mind, and that perhaps she would not bother with lunch at all.

Andrew walked with her to the door and said uncertainly, 'You will be at Mother's on Sunday, won't you?'

What for? Sorrel longed to say. So that I can play gooseberry?

She couldn't deceive herself any longer. Andrew had as little desire for her as she did for him, and the thought of them actually getting married was a complete farce.

Furious with herself and the rest of the world, and in particular one disruptive and Australian member of it, she hurried back to her car.

On her way she had to pass the dress-shop, and on some impulse she refused to name she went inside and asked the assistant if they had the dress in her size.

They had, and it fitted her as though designed for her. Heaven alone knew what folly was driving her, but she knew she was going to buy it, and moreover that she was going to wear it tonight when Val took them all out.

Rebelliously she wrote out the cheque for a heart-shakingly large amount, but it would be worth it when Val...

When Val what? she asked herself bleakly as she walked listlessly back to her car, her mood of angry euphoria deserting her, leaving her feeling cold and miserable as she was forced to confront the truth.

She couldn't hide behind the protection of her engagement to Andrew any longer. Oh, she would have lunch with his mother on Sunday, and then after a discreetly suitable interval, probably during one of their Friday evening dinners, once Val was safely off the scene, she would tell him that she thought they had made a mistake. He would argue with her, of course, but in the end he would not quite be able to hide his relief. Then one day she would hear from mutual friends that he and Jane were getting married.

She sighed faintly, wishing she could feel more real sorrow, more intense emotion, but she couldn't. Andrew didn't arouse her to one fraction of the intensity of feeling that Val could conjure up simply by being Val. He had been right about her engagement, but she wasn't going to let him know it. She couldn't bear to see the look in his eyes, to know... to know what?

In order to distract herself, she tried to imagine what she would have felt like if Val had been her fiancé, and she had found him with Jane...both of them so engrossed in one another, so obviously right for one another...

She stood still in the street as the pain hit her, clutching her dress-box in her arms, oblivious to the angry glower of the woman who almost walked into her, her eyes wild with anguish.

She loved him. She loved Val. She loved him, and if he asked it of her she would throw all her caution and her fear to the four winds, and give him whatever he should desire from her.

But he wouldn't ask. To him, she was simply a brief diversion to amuse him for a moment out of time. She tried not to think of the beautiful girls in Australia who must flock round him...tried not to allow herself to imagine how dull he must find her in comparison.

Not so dull that he hadn't desired her.

The world spun full circle and then stood still— and Sorrel spun with it, a slow heat burning through her body. Yes, he had desired her, and for a heartbeat of time in his arms she had teetered on the brink of overcoming her teenage fears and abandoning herself to the same fate as the rest of her sex. But sanity had intruded in time.

Val wasn't just a stranger who would pass out of her life, he was a member of her family, albeit a distant one, and he wouldn't want the complication of taking her as his lover. But if he did...

She stopped again, shivering in a fit of sensation that had nothing to do with the icy breeze. Now, when it was far, far too late, it wasn't fear she felt when she contemplated her memories of those two unknown and uninhibited lovers; it was envy. Envy for the pleasure that woman had known, envy for their freedom to express their desire, envy and the mature realisation that it had been her fear of the potential strength of *her own* desires that had frightened her.

Wearily, she got back into her car and started the engine, skidding over the loose mud and debris-covered surface of the derelict land.

Every now and again there would be a spate of letters of complaint in the local papers saying that it ought to be properly levelled and tarmacked, but nothing ever seemed to happen. It was full of potholes and deep ruts and her car bounded protestingly as she sank down into one of them.

SHE MANAGED to get her dress to her room without anyone seeing her. It left her shoulders bare and she hoped the hotel would be well-heated.

It hadn't been open very long; a small country house which had been taken over by a young couple who had turned it into a small hotel. There had been a rave write-up on it in the local papers. The bedrooms had been revamped in authentic period detail, apart from the addition of modern bathrooms, the dining-room was small and intimate, the menu out of this world—and those who had sampled its delights were full of praise for everything that had been done.

The Friday evening dinner dances were a new departure, and Sorrel wondered what it would be like. Even her father had been persuaded to go, complaining that he should by rights be with his ewes and that if he had known he was going to have to wear his dinner-suit there was no way he would have allowed himself to be persuaded to go.

But underneath his gruff exterior her father loved her mother very deeply, Sorrel knew, and she was so excited at the thought of the treat that Sorrel suspected nothing would have stopped her father from taking her.

The hotel was ten miles away and, mindful of the drink-driving laws, Simon had suggested they travel in two taxis.

Sorrel, who had had second thoughts at the last minute about the wisdom of appearing in a new dress, bearing in mind Simon's possible teasing, had put it on one side and dressed instead in the only other thing she had which was suitable: a plain black dress which she had bought in a mood of desperation because she had nothing to wear for Andrew's mother's traditional New Year's Eve party.

The dress hadn't been cheap, but it did very little for her, although black was normally a colour she could wear quite well. Perhaps it had something to do with the fact that this one was a full size too large, and really too plain to qualify for an evening dress.

It was more of a Jane dress than a Sorrel one, she acknowledged, looking at her reflection and seeing in her mirror an almost waif-like, dull creature who no man in his right mind would call attractive.

Angrily she tugged the dress off and reached for her new one. It left her arms and shoulders bare, the rich colour giving her skin an almost iridescent glow.

The silk shaped the curves of her body, giving them an alluring femininity that drew attention to her tiny waist and long legs.

She checked her make-up. Her eyes seemed more slumbrously green, and she frowned, wondering at the unusual fullness of her lips, almost as though they had just been kissed, or wanted to be kissed.

'Sorrel, taxis are here,' Simon called outside her room, and it was too late to change her mind and go back to her dull black.

She picked up the evening jacket she had knitted for herself almost four years ago in soft white mohair. It had a hood for extra warmth, and satin appliqué on the shoulders.

She had designed it herself, and after wearing it had been besieged with orders for others. It was still one of her best-selling designs, and only the previous winter she had been commissioned to turn it into a full-length cloak for a bride to wear over her dress.

'Come on,' Simon roared, and grabbing her evening bag Sorrel hurried to the door.

'You'd better travel with Val,' Simon told her, almost pushing her outside and into one of the waiting taxis before she could think of a practical excuse.

The door slammed behind her as she sat down, conscious of Val in the darkness of the car in a way that made her senses prickle warily.

Her heart almost stopped beating as the taxi moved and the interior was illuminated briefly by the farm's outside lights. If she had been very aware of Val's maleness in his jeans and woollen shirt, she was even more aware of it now, seeing him dressed elegantly in a dinner-suit that could never have been bought off the peg, and a white dress-shirt that made a breathtaking contrast to his tan.

Andrew frequently wore a dinner-suit, but he had never looked one tenth as suavely male in it as did Val.

'Something wrong?' he asked her solicitously, a disembodied voice from the opposite corner of the seat as they were plunged into darkness.

'No.'

'Mm ... Seen Andrew yet?'

Her scalp prickled atavistically. Had he *guessed* that she had been to see Andrew, or was he simply making polite conversation?

'Just briefly this morning.'

'To get his permission to come out with me to-night?'

His taunt took her breath away.

'Of course not,' she told him when she had got it back, adding grittily, 'For one thing, I don't need anyone's permission. And for another ... for another, I'm not going out with *you*, but with my family.'

'Ah, is that how you see it?' he murmured wickedly. 'Now, I have a very different perception of tonight. For me, taking your family out to dinner is a very welcome opportunity for me to hold you in my arms while I'm dancing with you. To...'

Sorrel prayed that the taxi driver couldn't hear him.

'Stop it, Val,' she demanded huskily. 'You know very well that you're just making that up. That...'

'Do I?' he muttered ironically.

Her heart pounded fiercely, but she ignored it. He was teasing her, that was all. It was his way of trying to jolt her out of her complacent rut and make her face what he considered to be reality. She believed now that his behaviour was well-intentioned, and of course he had no idea that she had been crazy enough to fall in love with him.

Fall in love with him? She bit down hard on her bottom lip to stop the frantic verbal outburst of denial she almost gave voice to.

It wasn't true! She couldn't let it be true, but of course she could not stop it, she acknowledged miserably, moments later. Why else was she reacting like...like a gauche teenager whenever he came near her? Why else was she suddenly finding fault with everything Andrew said and did—with her whole relationship with him? She had been happy enough before Val had stormed into her life, she reflected bitterly. Happy and content...and now she was neither. Now she was desperately in love with a man to whom she would never be anything other than his rather dull English relative.

'Tell me a bit more about this god-daughter of Andrew's mother's,' he demanded suddenly.

The question startled her, and she wondered nervously if he had, in that far too perceptive way of his, guessed the plans that Andrew's mother had for her son and Jane.

'Why?' she asked him, hiding her tension. 'Do you think she might be your type?'

He gave her a brief appraising look and then said softly, 'You're not *that* much of a fool, Sorrel, but it was a nice try.'

The car cornered sharply, throwing her helplessly against him. The impact of his hard body sent the breath rushing out of hers in a soft whoosh.

His hands steadied her, dark against the white of her jacket.

'You're not looking forward to this lunch on Sunday, are you? Why? Frightened he might ask too many awkward questions?'

'Such as?' she challenged him.

'Such as wanting to know how we spent those three days and nights up at the farmhouse, especially in view of the fact that it has only one bed, albeit a very large and comfortable double bed,' he added provocatively.

In the darkness, her face flamed with hectic colour, and she sent a brief helpless glance in the direction of the stoical driver. If he was listening to their conversation, he gave no sign of it.

'Andrew doesn't know about that,' she hissed softly. 'He hasn't been up to the farm since Uncle Giles left.'

'And you're not going to tell him, is that it? You're going to quietly pretend that nothing happened.'

'Nothing did happen,' Sorrel told him frantically, wondering if it was possible for him to hear the noisy thud of her heart. *She* certainly could, its erratic beat bearing all the tell-tale marks of her reaction to him.

'Like hell it didn't,' he told her inelegantly, stunning her with the biting force of his comment.

She could almost feel the emotional temperature between them rising, and her senses urged her to bring it down to normal before it became impossible.

'You never said how long you'd be able to stay,' she murmured, pulling away from him. 'Your business in London...'

'Can wait,' he told her succinctly. 'What's wrong, Sorrel? Frightened that I might not behave like a gentleman, that I might just tell that fiancé of yours...?'

'No,' she interrupted him shakily. 'No, Val, you can't do that.'

She almost told him that he was right and that she knew now that she couldn't marry Andrew, but pride held her back—pride and a certain deep-rooted vein of self-protection. If she admitted to him that she knew she couldn't marry Andrew, there was no saying what kind of questions he might start asking her.

She could see he was about to say something, but the taxi was turning off the road and the hotel was in front of them. She diverted his attention to it, and then filled the short ride down the drive with a stream of hectic chatter, determined not to let him get back on to the subject of her engagement.

'OH, MY GOODNESS, isn't this wonderful!' Amy Llewellyn was exclaiming when Sorrel emerged from the cloakroom to join the rest of the family in the reception area.

It was. No expense had been spared to return to the house the ambiance of an elegant country home.

The reception area was pleasantly large, with a log fire burning in the huge fireplace and attractive groups of tables and chairs close to it.

'The dining-room's this way,' a smiling waiter told them, indicating a door off to one side of the room.

During the daytime it must have wonderful views over the gardens, Sorrel reflected as they were shown to their table, but now the rich damask curtains were drawn against the chilly March night, and a fire just as welcoming as the one outside burned in an enormous Adam grate.

The dining-room was comfortably full, the low hum of people's conversation swirling enticingly around them as they all sat down. The tables were round, the linen white and immaculately starched. The dining-room was decorated in deep crimson with bold touches of dark greens and blues. None of them, it seemed, required an appetiser, although Sorrel did notice Val saying something to the wine waiter.

When he returned with an ice-bucket and a magnum of champagne, she looked questioningly at Val.

'This won't rival your elderberry wine,' he told her mother wickedly, 'but I think it's appropriate to drink a toast to the Llewellyn family, whichever side of the world it lives on.'

That toast seemed to set the mood for the evening, which was full of reminiscences about various points of mutual family history, with Val telling them far more about the details of his antecedents than he had done before.

It seemed that the Australian Llewellyns were very conscious of their Welsh heritage, and Val admitted that it had always been an ambition of his father's to visit Wales.

'Oh, they must come over!' Sorrel heard her mother exclaiming impulsively. 'During the summer. They could stay with us...I'd love to meet the rest of your family, Val.'

'They aren't as nice as me,' he told her solemnly, and they all laughed, even Sorrel, but the time for laughter was gone when they had finished eating and gone to sit in the drawing-room, where the parquet floor had been cleared for dancing and a small band was playing on the raised dais at one end of the room.

Sorrel watched as her parents got up to dance, and then Simon and Fiona.

'Dance with me?' Val asked her quietly, and, much as she knew she was dreading going into his arms, she also knew that she had no choice.

It was every bit as bad as she had anticipated. He was a good dancer, and every movement of his body invited hers to move with it, surrendering itself to the spell he was weaving over her. She fought to resist, holding her body stiffly resistant, keeping as much distance between them as she could.

'Has anyone ever told you how much this colour suits you?' Val whispered against her hair. She missed a step and half stumbled, allowing him to gather her up against him. The sensation of his hand against the bare flesh of her back made her shiver and then curse as the music changed and the band started playing a slow, evocative number, the lights going down and the couples on the floor swaying together, cloaked in the intimacy of the darkness and the music.

'I've never seen skin like yours before,' Val told her. 'It's like mother-of-pearl.' His fingertip traced a line along her collarbone, and she shuddered, gasping as he bent his head and bit gently at her flesh.

'How easily do you bruise, Sorrel?' he muttered thickly against her throat, while she looked round wildly, praying that none of her family could see them. What he was doing to her was making her weak to her knees. If he hadn't been holding her, she suspected she would have slid to the floor in a melted puddle of flesh and bones.

'I'd love to leave my mark on you for that complacent idiot to see. Do you know that?' he added roughly, silencing the protest she had been about to utter as her body responded shockingly to his touch.

'Has he ever kissed you like this?' he asked her, and as though he knew the answer he bit almost savagely at her skin, making her stifle a soft sound of pain.

It was unfair that he should torment her like this, practically making love to her while they danced, holding her in such a way that he was... She tensed suddenly, her eyes widening as she felt the sudden stirring of his body. This was no artifice, no game, she acknowledged painfully, knowing that her face was flushed and her breath coming too quickly; but the way he was holding her, the hot, predatory look in his eyes, the movements of his body against hers, each one of them making her intimately aware of his arousal, were things she could not ignore.

The music stopped and she started to pull away from him, but he held on to her and said sharply, 'No.'

She gave him a frantic questioning look and he said roughly, 'For heaven's sake, Sorrel, I can't go back and join the rest of your family, without them knowing...'

He didn't need to say more. A scalding wave of colour washed her skin, and he took advantage of her confusion to grip hold of her arm and walk her across the floor towards the door.

'What are you *doing?*' she asked him angrily. 'We can't just walk out.'

'You're thirsty. You wanted a drink.'

'The waiter could have brought us one.'

Another couple reached the door from the opposite side, and Val pulled her in front of him to make way for them, holding her there against his body so that she could feel the heat. He was still aroused, and that knowledge made her objections die away.

'What's the matter?' he asked her when the other couple had gone. 'Have you never experienced the same kind of embarrassing incidents with Andrew? But of course you haven't,' he taunted her. 'Andrew is far too much a gentleman to ever dream of forgetting himself in such a way. Isn't that what you're going to tell me? Well, I'll tell *you* something, Sorrel. When you're lying in bed with that husband of yours, you're going to remember tonight and you're going to wish like hell for...'

'Stop it,' she begged him in a choking voice. 'I won't listen to any more.' And she would have pulled away from him and left him there if he hadn't constrained her.

'Come on, you two. Dad's ordered another magnum. He wants to drink your health, Val,' Simon announced, suddenly materialising at their side, his smile fading as he saw their faces. 'What's wrong?' he asked.

'Nothing,' Val assured him, adding quietly, 'Look, just give us a couple of minutes, will you? And then we'll rejoin you.' He saw that Simon was looking uncertainly towards their table, and told him frankly, 'Your sister has the knack of reminding me that I'm only human.'

And Sorrel flushed as she saw the enlightenment dawn in Simon's eyes, followed by distinct amusement.

'Ah, yes,' he agreed, ignoring the furious looks Sorrel was sending him. 'I know exactly what you mean.'

And he sauntered off, leaving Sorrel to round angrily on Val and demand breathlessly, 'How could you do that? How could you...'

'I didn't have much option,' Val told her drily. 'He looked as though he was about to drag us back to the table by force. Now that *would* have been embarrassing, don't you agree?'

'But now he'll know...he'll think...'

'That I find you physically desirable?' Val asked her, looking at her. 'What makes you think he doesn't already?'

And that comment *did* take her breath away. What was Val saying? That he found her physically attractive, that he desired her, and that moreover Simon knew it? She looked up at Val, but his face was shuttered, his eyes coolly remote, as though he was regretting what he had said.

She wondered if he was afraid that she might read more into his admission than there was. That she might be foolish enough to imagine that, because he wanted her on a physical level, he must love her as well.

With a little pang, she wondered if she ought to put his mind at rest and assure him that he was quite safe, that she wasn't quite that much of an idiot, even if she had been silly enough to fall in love with him.

CHAPTER NINE

'WELL, it's today you're having lunch with Andrew's mother, isn't it?' Simon commented at breakfast on Sunday. 'I don't envy you.'

'So you've already said,' Sorrel reminded him tartly.

She had been prickly and on edge ever since the night of the dinner dance, alternately praying that Val would announce that he was going to leave and hoping that he would stay. She was on an emotional seesaw that left her illuminatingly aware of how very right she had been to fear the strength of her own feelings.

Now her mother was trying to persuade Val to stay on until Uncle Giles returned from Cardiff, and that was not until the middle of next week.

A phone call had been made to Australia with Val's connivance, and all of them, including Sorrel herself, had been persuaded to speak to their Australian relatives, who apparently were in the habit of gathering together on Saturday afternoons. Her mother had suggested that Val might want to have the privacy of speaking to his family alone, but he had vetoed this idea, had almost seemed apprehensive of it, Sorrel recognised.

His sisters, far from seeming as formidable as she had feared, had talked eagerly of them all getting together, and now it seemed a fair probability that some form of gathering would be organised.

Even her father had become suddenly garrulous under the influence of the excitement, and now, abruptly, out of the blue he commented, 'I knew there was something I meant to ask you, Val...' All of them waited expectantly.

'Do you remember, Amy?' he asked. 'It's mentioned in one of the diaries. I forget which one now, but there was definitely something about a relative coming back from Australia.'

'Yes, of course! Heavens, how could I have forgotten that?' Sorrel's mother chimed in. 'I remember at the time thinking how romantic it all was. You must have read it, Sorrel,' she began, turning to where Sorrel was sitting. Then she checked and said thoughtfully, 'But maybe not. Don't you remember, Dan, that diary was the one that your father spilled tea on? Sorrel would only have been about seven or so at the time.'

'Lord, yes. Ma was furious, wasn't she?'

'Would one of you mind translating, for the benefit of those of us who are completely fogbound?' Simon interrupted them humorously.

Sorrel's mother laughed, turning to Val to say, 'One of the diaries made mention of a young Australian coming to the farm. There were vague hints of him having been something of a black sheep, but Marsha, the girl who wrote the diary, wrote that he had come back home to claim her sister as his bride. Apparently there'd been a secret understanding between them, despite the fact that he was actually transported. She'd waited for him. And he took her back to Australia with him in the teeth of her parents' opposition, and Marsha's father told her that if she went he would disown her...' She broke off and looked at Val. 'Good heavens, do you suppose that's why there's never been any communication between the two families?'

'It sounds like it,' Val confirmed. 'We have the other side of the story, though. How my ancestor was transported for stealing a loaf of bread to feed his starving brothers and sisters, and how he was lucky enough to be bonded to a reasonable master. After he'd served his seven years' indenture, he was set free. According to *our* family diaries, he won enough money gambling to sail back to Wales, but once he got there he realised that he could never settle, and that somehow or other his home had become too small and narrow for him. Very circumspect, our ancestors. There was no mention of disapproval in *our* diaries, just the blissful ravings of a new wife, who came to love Australia as much as her husband did. That and the start of a tradition that...'

He broke off suddenly, looking rather bleak, while Amy Llewellyn, not noticing, said eagerly, 'Oh, don't stop there, Val. What tradition?'

'Oh, it's nothing really, and it doesn't mean a thing. It's just that, by chance really, the eldest sons of our families have always married girls from home.'

'Home?' Sorrel queried sharply. 'You mean... here...Britain? But you said your mother was Russian.'

'She *is*, but my father met her over here while he was at university. She's English by birth, even though she has Russian antecedents. White Russian,' he explained. 'Her grandparents were émigrés, having fled from the Russian revolution. I believe there was a whole community of Russians living in London at one time.'

'Yes. That's true,' Sorrel's mother agreed. 'Heavens, how interesting and romantic. Well, Val,' she looked expectantly at him, 'do you think you will continue the tradition and take an English bride home with you?'

'Not this trip,' he said curtly.

Sorrel got up from the table, a feeling of shocked misery making her insides ache. Ever since Friday night Val had been distant with her, no longer teasing her, tending to spend most of his time with Si-

mon and her father. She tried to pretend that she
didn't mind, that it was for the best, but she missed
the warm intimacy she had shared with him, and
her loneliness was just a foretaste of what she would
actually experience once he was really gone, she
knew.

She prepared for her lunch date with Andrew's
mother without any real enthusiasm. Simon and
Fiona were going out for the afternoon to see some
friends, and she watched enviously from her bedroom window as she saw them walking across the
yard arm in arm. They had invited Val to go with
them, but he had declined. He had become notice-
ably withdrawn, or so it seemed to Sorrel; a faintly
austere look about him that she would never have
originally associated with the tormentingly outrageous character he had seemed to be at first. But
now she had come to realise that there were hidden
and deceptive aspects to Val. She wondered if any
woman had ever really known him...or ever would.

She saw Simon and Fiona drive away, and acknowledged that if she didn't leave soon she was
going to be late. Just for a moment she contemplated not going, but knew she was being a coward. Squaring her shoulders, she picked up her
jacket and went downstairs.

Val was standing in the yard when she walked
out, but since he ignored her she went towards her
car and got in, slamming the door.

The engine fired, and she slipped the car into gear, and then realised as she tried to drive away she had a flat tyre.

A flat tyre and no spare, she acknowledged grimly as she stopped the engine and got out. She would have to ask her mother if she could borrow her car. Her tyre must have had a slow puncture, probably caused that day in the car park.

Sighing faintly, she started to hurry back to the house.

'What's wrong?' Val asked her, walking into the yard. 'Changed your mind?'

'No, I have not,' she told him tiredly. 'If you must know, I've got a flat tyre. I'll have to ask Ma if I can use her car.'

'No need. I'll drive you there,' he offered laconically.

She wanted to refuse, but couldn't think of a good enough reason. Time was ticking away and she was already in a mild state of panic, knowing Andrew's mother's obsession with good timekeeping.

'Well, if you're sure you don't mind—' she began doubtfully. Commanding her not to be a fool, Val told her to get in the car while he told her parents where he was going.

He looked surprisingly grim when he rejoined her and started the engine of his hired Ford.

'You're not going to listen to what *anyone* tells you are you, Sorrel?' he demanded as he drove out of the yard. 'You're going to go ahead and destroy your life by marrying him.'

Sorrel looked away from him. She desperately wanted to admit the truth, but she couldn't. If she did...

'Hell,' she heard him saying thickly, 'I ought to take you and shake you until your spine rattles. How *can* you be such a fool?'

'For what, preferring Andrew to you?' she challenged him hotly, appalled by her own folly the moment she realised what she had said.

Immediately she froze, wishing herself a thousand miles away, but for once Val didn't seem to realise the opening she had given him because, instead of making the kind of retort she was expecting, he simply looked at her in a way that made her body shiver in nervous awareness of the fact that beneath that controlled exterior there lurked a temper which, if it ever exploded, could rage dangerously out of control.

'Which way?' he asked her curtly, and it was several seconds before she realised he was asking her for directions. She gave them shakily, wishing to heaven she had not accepted his offer of a lift. The atmosphere inside the car was explosive to the point where she wouldn't have been remotely surprised to see it bursting into spontaneous combustion.

They were half-way there when Val who, like her, had maintained the taut silence during the journey, suddenly asked her harshly, 'Would you like me to pick you up, or will *he* bring you back?'

'He' meant Andrew, of course. *Would* Andrew drive her home, or would he be too concerned about 'dear Jane' to worry about her? She suspected that she already knew the answer to that one, but her pride wouldn't let her admit it to Val.

'I'll make my own arrangements,' she told him stiffly.

'Really, and what will they be?' he asked her cuttingly. 'A detour to his flat so that you can prove to him that "nothing happened" between us. I may not have taken your virginity, Sorrel, but if I had wanted to...'

Sorrel could hardly believe what she was hearing. Her self-control went up in flames as her temper overcame her good sense.

'Right, that's it!' she told him stormily. 'I've had enough. You can just stop right here. I'm not going another mile with you. I'm tired of your innuendoes, of you making fun of me. All right, so I am a virgin. So what? I realise it makes me into some kind of freak. Something to be avoided at all costs.'

She didn't get any further. To her shock, Val pulled abruptly off the road and on to the muddy

verge. It was only a narrow country lane, and there
was no other traffic. She would have a long walk if
he took her at her word and threw her out, she recognised wildly—and she would certainly be late for
lunch. For some reason, that made her want to
laugh, a hysterical high-pitched sound, which she
suppressed as soon as it bubbled up in her throat.

'To hell with your damn virginity!' Val was saying, and before she could react he had taken hold
of her and pulled her into his arms, his fingers biting into her as she hung dizzily between disbelief
and wonderment at the look she saw in his eyes.

'I want you, Sorrel,' he muttered against her
mouth. 'I want you and by heaven, if you were
mine you wouldn't be untouched ... unloved ...'

His voice faded, the sound smothered by his
mouth as it brushed tormentingly against her own,
back and forth, until she was desperate to hold on
to him and keep his mouth on hers and hold it
there.

She couldn't help it. She clung to him, her fingers burrowing beneath the tweed jacket he was
wearing to the cloth covering the solid muscles of
his back.

Beneath his mouth, she made a sound that was
half a protest and half an acknowledgement of her
need, and then there was no more thought, no more
anything other than the feeling that was pouring
through her as he answered her unspoken pleas and

held her mouth beneath his own. His tongue
opened her lips and she trembled wildly. She tensed
and he held on to her, his arms tense, a fierce
tremor seizing him, and he watched her as she felt
it, his eyes half closed, an odd smile curling his
mouth.

'You see,' he said unsteadily, not releasing her. 'It
makes me as vulnerable as it does you. Don't be
afraid, Sorrel. Come to London with me,' he
begged her, his eyes suddenly dark. 'Let me show
you...'

Show her what? How much he would hurt her
when he eventually grew tired of her? What a fool
she was.

'No,' she told him sharply, pulling out of his
arms, and shivering suddenly, her skin cold beneath her clothes.

'What just happened between us doesn't mean a
single damn to you, does it?' he demanded harshly,
the words bitten off and filled with acid anger.
'You've decided the way your life is going to be,
and you're not going to let anything change that.
You're going to marry Andrew, no matter what...
Well, I wish you joy of him, Sorrel, but I damn well
don't think you'll get any.'

And, with that, he put the car in motion with
jerky movements so at odds with his normal grace.
Apart from giving him terse necessary directions,
Sorrel remained silent.

He might want her now; but that didn't mean anything other than that he was a man used to having what he wanted. Wanting wasn't enough for her, anyway. She needed more than that. Oh, he could bemuse and entice her with the desire he could conjure up in her body, but there would come a time when desire wasn't enough, when she would hate him for his physical dominance of her, and herself for allowing it when she knew that desire was all he felt for her.

'You can drop me here,' she told him when they got to the bottom of the drive that led to Andrew's mother's house. She was uncomfortably conscious of the fact that her lipstick was missing and her hair untidy, but she couldn't do anything about it...not with Val watching her with that cold air of contempt.

He ignored her comment and drove towards the house. As bad luck would have it, Jane, Andrew and Andrew's mother were all standing in the drive. Andrew and Jane must have just arrived, Sorrel recognised, and Andrew's mother was kissing Jane enthusiastically, in a way that she had never kissed her.

Val stopped the car, and she reached shakily for the doorhandle. She could see that Andrew was frowning as he looked at them, and that his mother was looking rather grim.

'Sorrel!' she exclaimed, coming forward. 'I suspect this must be your cousin.' Her smile grew even grimmer as Sorrel's eyes betrayed her wary surprise that she knew who Val was. 'I saw your brother in Ludlow the other day. He told me all about your Australian visitor.'

Something in the way she said the words 'all about' made Sorrel's heart drop. What on earth had Simon been saying? He had promised her...

She felt Val's presence behind her and, despite their quarrel, was glad of it, especially when she saw the unhappy, defensive way in which Andrew was avoiding meeting her eyes. Jane looked smug and just a little triumphant, and her feeling of disquiet grew.

'I must say I was rather surprised to hear that the two of you spent three whole days together *alone,*' Andrew's mother commented critically, ignoring Sorrel's attempt to introduce Val to her. 'Not quite the sort of thing one expects to hear, but I suppose...'

Wondering what on earth she was supposed to say, Sorrel fumed bitterly that Simon couldn't have caused more trouble for her if he had deliberately planned it that way. She felt like someone on trial and already prejudged by both judge and jury, and she was just wondering what on earth she was going to say when she was appalled to hear Val murmuring laconically behind her, 'It's not the days they ought to be worrying about it, is it, Sorrel? It's the three nights we spent sharing the same bed.'

His words had the effect of a spaceman suddenly materialising in front of them. Sorrel wasn't sure who looked the most stunned. An unpleasant flush was beginning to stain Andrew's mother's face, although why *she* should look so angry, when surely Val had just confirmed for her everything that she had hoped to hear, Sorrel couldn't understand.

Andrew looked frankly dumbfounded, his eyes bulging a little as he stared accusingly at her. Strange that she had never noticed his similarity to a frog before, she thought half hysterically.

Certainly a frog that would never turn into a prince, no matter how much she kissed him, while Jane... Well, Jane was giving Andrew sickeningly compassionate looks of sympathy, her eyes self-righteously averted from Sorrel's face.

No doubt she can't bring herself to look at a fallen woman, Sorrel thought savagely.

'We had to, you see,' Val continued chattily, as though completely oblivious to the reactions of his audience. 'There was only the one bed, and only one set of bedding. Not that *I* minded.' He looked across at Andrew and remarked conversationally, 'But then, I suppose I don't need to tell you what a pleasure it is to sleep with Sorrel in your arms.'

Sorrel could hardly believe it. Andrew goggled, looking even more frog-like, and cast an imploring look at his mother.

'Sorrel and I have never slept together,' he announced, stuttering, but he sounded more like a little boy denying a petty crime than a man making a positive statement, Sorrel noticed.

'I should think not,' his mother agreed. Andrew's mother was a large woman with a tendency towards rather too high colouring. Her flushed face did not go well with the mauve tweed skirt she had chosen to wear, Sorrel reflected unkindly. She knew she ought to be feeling humiliated beyond all bearing, but instead she was having to control an appalling urge to laugh. The whole thing was too much like an incredible farce. There was Andrew, fervently denying any physical relationship between them. There was Jane, all bashful blushes and shocked eyes, like the heroine out of a Victorian novelette, and almost in confirmation of her thoughts Sorrel saw Andrew's mother turn to her son and say commandingly, 'Andrew, I think you'd better take Jane inside. I'm sure she is as shocked as I am at what we've just heard.' She pursed her lips. 'Of course, I can't say I'm surprised. I've always told Andrew that you had a wild streak, Sorrel. I couldn't believe it when your brother told me what had happened.'

Oh, yes, you could, Sorrel thought bitterly. You were only too pleased to believe it. But she kept that thought to herself and said coldly instead, 'Good, because while it's true that Val and I did spend two nights sharing the same bed, I'm as virginal after those two nights as I was before them. More's the pity,' she added grimly, as much to her own shock as everyone else's.

Even Val looked slightly astounded, and no wonder, she reflected, a sudden sickening sensation of having well and truly burned her boats overwhelming her. Caution warned her to back down before she committed any further indiscretions, but another part of her refused to listen.

She turned to Andrew and told him curtly, 'There's no need to worry, Andrew. I'd already decided to tell you that I felt it best that we ended our engagement.' She saw the relief and triumph in his mother's eyes and told her, 'Yes, you're pleased, aren't you? Now he can marry *your* choice. Well, I hope she's more capable of arousing him than I was, otherwise you'll be whistling for your grandchildren.'

There was a concerted shocked gasp from mother and son. Sorrel was shaking from head to foot, no longer really aware of what she was saying or doing.

She turned to Val and said bitterly, 'Happy now, are you?' And then she started to run down the drive, reaction setting in and tears pouring from her eyes.

Behind her she heard Val call out something, and then the hard pounding of his feet behind her.

He overtook her just as she reached the car, wrenching open the door and bundling her inside. When she tried to get out he stopped her, almost hurting her as he pushed her into her seat and locked the door.

They drove in silence, until Sorrel realised abruptly that he wasn't taking her home.

'Where are we going?' she demanded huskily.

'Where do you think?'

The farm. He was taking her back to Wales! She gave a tiny shiver, almost as though part of her recognised the inevitability of what must happen. She ought to stop him ... to say something, but she didn't. She just sat there, numb with reaction.

CHAPTER TEN

IT WAS a long drive to the cottage. Far too long for
Sorrel, sitting at Val's side with nothing else to do
but go over and over in her mind that horrible in-
terlude with Andrew and his family.

And what she had hated most about it, she recognised miserably, had not been Andrew's defec-
tion, but that Val should witness it. That *Val* should
see the true nature of the man she had been prepared to commit her life to.

Andrew hadn't even had the guts to break off
their relationship himself. He had let his mother do
it for him.

She shivered, remembering the look of gloating
pleasure in Andrew's mother's eyes after Val had
made his announcement. If only Andrew had spoken up for her then, if only he had silenced his
mother and said that it was something the two of
them could discuss in private... or, even more unlikely, if only he had simply taken her hand and said
that he trusted her, that he had faith in her.

Val would never have allowed anyone to humili-
ate the woman he loved as she had just been hu-

miliated, and for no reason at all tears clogged her throat and trickled saltily from her eyes.

They were travelling in a fast stream of traffic with no opportunity for Val to stop. She heard him swear under his breath, and a large white handkerchief was thrust in her direction, accompanied by a grim, 'He's not worth it. Hell, he didn't even *try* to defend you.'

'How could he, after what you'd said?' Sorrel demanded shakily. 'You wanted it to happen. You knew...'

'What? What did I know, Sorrel? That he didn't give a single damn about you? Yes, I knew it, and if you'd had any sense you'd have known it too.'

She *had* known it, of course, but she couldn't *tell* him that.

'A year from now you'll be thanking me for doing you a favour,' he added curtly.

'A *year* from now?' Her voice was bitter. 'And in the meantime, what am I supposed to do, Val? Ludlow's a small place. How do you think I'm going to feel knowing people will be gossiping, believing that Andrew broke our engagement because you and I were lovers?'

'There's an easy solution to that,' he told her equably. 'Come back to Perth with me.'

She froze and stared at him. He was concentrating on the traffic, his eyes slightly narrowed. Had she really heard him say that, or was she imagining things?

'It will do you good ... broaden your horizons,' he told her. 'You can stay with my parents. My mother will enjoy having someone to fuss over, and Perth's full of men who will be only too glad to help you forget him.'

The fierce shock of delight left her. For a second she had imagined... What? That he was inviting her to go back to Perth with him as his lover? Hardly; he had just made that quite clear. What he was offering was a family visit. An excuse to get away from Ludlow and sample another kind of life. In other circumstances, if she had been capable of merely seeing him as a distant relative, she would have jumped at the suggestion, but loving him as she did ...

'We need petrol,' he told her abruptly, pulling into a garage. Sorrel wondered if she ought to get out of the car and make a scene, demanding to be taken home. She had no idea why he was insisting on taking her to the cottage. Perhaps he intended to keep her there until she agreed to go back to Perth with him. She was beginning to think he was capable of doing it. Look at the ruthless way he had destroyed her engagement.

The fact that she had spent three days at the farm alone with him would be all over Ludlow within hours. Andrew's mother would see to that, and the story would no doubt have the kind of insidious embellishment to it that would make it impossible for her to tell anyone the truth. They would all assume that...that she and Val were lovers. Her face flamed as she remembered what she had said about her virginity. What on earth had possessed her?

She watched Val walking back to the car. The wind whipped the dark hair sleekly against his scalp. He moved quickly and easily, like a man used to wide open spaces.

'I've rung your mother and told her what's happened,' he announced briefly as he got into the car and started the engine.

'You've what? Have you *also* told her you've kidnapped me?' she asked him sardonically.

He gave her an unfathomable look and said quietly, 'You and I have some unfinished business to deal with,' but he wouldn't say any more and soon they were leaving the rest of the traffic behind, climbing up into the hills, whose sides were barren and bare under the lash of the March wind.

The snow had gone, apart from that covering the tops of the distant mountains. Val drove into the yard and parked the car with easy familiarity, going round to her door to open it for her.

She shivered as the wind buffeted her. Her thin lambswool jumper and pleated skirt were not designed for such an exposed environment. Nor were her high-heeled shoes, she acknowledged as she pulled away from Val and tried to hurry across the yard.

The cobblestones trapped her heels and she went over on one ankle, crying out sharply.

'Idiotic things,' Val growled, picking her up and carrying her the rest of the way to the door. 'Why the hell are you wearing them?'

'Because *if* you remember, I was on my way to lunch with my prospective mother-in-law...my *ex*-prospective mother-in-law, she added as he put her down and opened the door.

The cottage felt chilly and she shivered, hugging her arms round her body, trying to ward off the cold.

'I'll light the range,' Val told her, disappearing in the direction of one of the outhouses.

She watched him listlessly. It was as though that terrible scene with Andrew and his mother had robbed her of all energy and will-power. Instead of formulating her own decisions... It was all too much of an effort to make her own decisions; it was much easier to let someone else do it for her.

Val came back and she watched him lighting the fire. He had large, capable hands that dealt efficiently with the firelighters and coal, and then adjusted the range to get the proper draught.

'There, I think it will be OK now.'

'Aren't you going to light the one upstairs?' she asked him uninterestedly, and earned herself a sharp look.

'Do you want me to?'

Something in the soft words evoked a shudder of sensation deep inside her body, but she was too emotionally weary to worry about it.

She gave a tired shrug and went to look out of the window.

'Since when has what *I* wanted influenced you?' she asked him.

He came up behind her, and in the window she saw him lift his hands as though to take hold of her. She held her breath, not sure whether to be glad or sorry when they fell to his sides.

'You blame me for what happened with Andrew...'

She gave a mirthless laugh. 'Are you trying to say that you *didn't* deliberately plan the whole thing? You and Simon between you?'

'It was for your own good, Sorrel,' he told her, not making any attempt to deny it.

'My own good?' Hysteria coloured her voice. 'What was? The humiliation of having Andrew's mother virtually tell me I was a ... a whore ...' She saw him wince. 'Do you realise what you've done?'

She turned away from him, shaking violently, and then said in an impassioned voice, 'For your information, I had already decided to bring my en-

gagement with Andrew to an end.' She saw the
fierce light burn in his eyes and stepped back from
him, her own eyes shadowing warily.

'So you see, it was all quite unnecessary. I went
to see Andrew the other day at the shop. Jane was
there. When I saw them together, I realised then
that she would make him a far better wife than I
ever could.'

She raised her head and frowned as she saw the
light die out of his eyes.

He took hold of her and shook her roughly. 'You
little fool! Even now you're still putting his needs
before your own, aren't you? Aren't you? If you
hadn't seen him with her, you'd have gone on with
it . . . sacrificing yourself.'

'Sacrificing myself? I *wanted* to marry him, remember.'

'Yes, I remember,' he told her grimly. 'And I also
remember hearing you tell his mother that you
wished that I had taken your virginity during those
nights we spent together.'

She opened her mouth to deny it, but the words
wouldn't come. Now it was there between them,
almost a presence in the room with them. She could
feel it beating at the defences of her mind and body,
impelling her onwards, past the safety barriers she
had erected around her emotions.

'Was that true, Sorrel?' he asked her softly. '*Do*
you wish that I'd been your lover?'

All she had to do was to say no. He wouldn't force her. He wasn't that sort of man.

She moistened her lips, but the denial wouldn't come.

'Is that why you brought me here, to make love to me...as a consolation prize for losing Andrew?'

She had pushed him too far, she saw in the split-second darkening of his eyes and the rage that burned in them.

He muttered something bitingly sarcastic under his breath and took hold of her. 'I brought you here because I thought you needed time to... to adjust to what has happened. The thought of making love to you was the last thing on my mind. For Pete's sake, just what do you think I am?' He saw the look in her eyes and said with sudden savagery, 'All right then, since you think it of me anyway, I might as well fulfil your worst expectations, mightn't I?

THE BEDROOM was as they'd left it; the quilt neatly folded, the bed stripped, the hearth empty. Simon had been so anxious to get them safely home that they hadn't bothered packing the bedding into the Land Rover.

'Not exactly the romantic venue it was,' he told her angrily. 'No comfortable darkness to hide the lies we're going to tell one another. No bright fire flames to warm the coldness of lovemaking without love, but for all that, Sorrel, I promise you I'll give you a taste of pleasure that you will never, never forget. Unless, of course, you want me to stop.'

Of course she wanted him to stop. She didn't want him to touch her like this, in anger and guilt, out of some misguided belief that he owed her something for what he had done. And yet, even as one half of her acknowledged these thoughts, another part which was fiercer, more bitter, more tormented by everything that had happened, demanded reparation, urged her on down a path of self-destruction from which there could be no going back.

'No, I'm not going to ask you to stop,' she told him proudly. 'You owe me this, Val. You've destroyed my life, my future. I was happy with what I had, but you weren't. You didn't care that I was content, so you decided in your arrogance to take what I had away from me. And now there's nothing. Add to that the fact that I'm a virgin at twenty-four, and it shouldn't be too hard for you to see what you've done to me.

'Who's going to want me now, once they know the truth? How many men do *you* know who'd want a woman of my age, totally without any kind of sexual experience? Or am I supposed to lie to them? To let them believe otherwise, until it's too late?' she asked him cynically.

'I don't want to spend the rest of my life alone,
Val. Eventually I shall want to marry, have children, and I can't do that while my virginity hangs
round my neck like a curse, making every man who
finds out about it wonder what the hell is wrong
with me.

'It's your fault that all this has happened, so it
seems only fair that you should be the one to give
me my freedom, doesn't it?' she said quietly, and
her hands went to the buttons fastening her kilt-
style pleated skirt.

She saw his face drain of colour, and had a moment of savage satisfaction. She had got to him
now, made him realise just what he had done with
his meddling. For the first time she saw him looking hesitant and unsure.

'What's wrong?' she goaded him. 'Is it too much
to ask, after all? You said you desired me,' she told
him flatly. 'Then prove it to me, Val.'

Something in her face snapped his self-control,
and he reached for her, saying fiercely, 'Oh, I will.'
And then it was his hands and not hers that were
removing her clothes, and then his own, the last
cold, clear light of the March day illuminating the
golden beauty of his body.

Unlike her, he didn't seem to be embarrassed by
his nudity, nor chilled by the coldness of the room.
He saw her glance flicker to the bed, and he reached
for the quilt, spreading it on the mattress.

'You do want it like this, don't you?' he asked her with exquisite and very distant politeness. 'Out in the open, without any concealing shadows.'

At first she thought he was making a taunting allusion to her teenage experience, but she realised she was wrong when he continued savagely, 'After all, it isn't as though we're going to need any comforting shadows to cloak the intensity of our emotions, is it? Because there won't be any emotion. I thought I knew you, but I didn't. I didn't know you at all. I thought you were vulnerable... tender...'

He drew a shaky breath and she steeled herself against her hurt.

Yes, she was all of those things and more, but he had driven her to inflict this punishment on both of them, and she wasn't going to draw back now, not to save her pride or his.

'What's wrong?' she asked him coldly, giving him a significant look. 'Worried that you might not be able to?'

'To what?' he asked her acidly, coming round the side of the bed and grabbing hold of her, his hands hard against her waist and hips as he moved deliberately against her.

'To what?' he demanded again, letting her feel the power of his sexual arousal while he bent his head and said something so cruelly explicit in her ear that she shivered with the coldness that touched her heart.

'I learned a long time ago to take advantage of the opportunities that life offers,' he told her grimly. 'I told you that when I worked as a geologist, the opportunity to indulge in feminine companionship was rare and had to be made the most of. Don't worry, Sorrel, I won't be the one to back down.'

And neither would she, she promised herself hardily, refusing to give in to the slow, burning throb of sickness that was gradually invading her body, as the shock of the scene with Andrew faded and fear took its place.

Val felt the tiny shudder that tormented her and said mockingly, 'Having second thoughts?'

She shook her head, but she couldn't look at him. Held like this in his arms, in what was a cruel parody of a lovers' embrace, while her body remained chilled and unaroused, was bringing home to her the enormity of what she had done. And it was all her own fault. She had goaded and tormented him, deliberately driven him. And now, when the reality of what she had done was making her hurt as she had never hurt before, it was too late to draw back.

'We'd better get it over with then, hadn't we?' he said silkily. One hand left her body and clasped the back of her neck, his fingers playing with her hair, almost as though he couldn't resist its silky feel.

'I'm a man who always pays his debts, Sorrel. Remember that.' And then his head came down and his mouth possessed hers with a cool insolence that made her weep inside as she remembered how it had been before. Her body, knowing how it was being insulted and short-changed, refused to relax and warm. His mouth was skilled and knowing, but it wasn't enough. When his hand cupped her breast, she tensed in protest, forgetting for a moment that it was herself who had instigated this. She trembled slightly as his fingers touched her flesh, aching to close her eyes as she looked into his and saw the cold indifference there, his attention moving from her face to her body, drawing hers with it, so that she was forced to watch the ultimate humiliation of seeing his fingertip draw slow circles around the peak of her breast. It should have aroused her. She wanted it to arouse her. She wanted to drown in self-contempt, so that when he was gone she could destroy the love she felt for him by reminding herself of this humiliation, but her body had a will of its own and refused to respond, her flesh as cold as his eyes. Her body knew the difference between desire given freely and that which was manufactured.

When his head lowered to her breast, she jerked away from him, unable to endure the thought of his touch. Tears of anguish and despair lodged in a solid lump at the back of her throat. He lifted his head and looked at her, his eyes remote.

'Do you want me to go on?' he asked her cordially.

She wanted to say yes. She wanted him to suffer the humiliation she was suffering, to know what it felt like to... But some spark of sanity intervened and she shook her had, unable to say the small word of denial.

There was no relief when he levered himself away from her body. No sensation of having made the right decision. Nothing but a vast blank nothingness, an intense feeling of failure and despair.

She lay motionless, staring at the ceiling, without blinking, aware of him getting dressed, but making no attempt to move. Perhaps if she lay here like this, fate would be kind and make it possible for her to slip away into some kind of protective permanent darkness. She heard him cross the floor and open the door, and her body shook with a dry sob. Downstairs she heard him open the back door and then the sound of the car starting. He was leaving her here. Well, she was safe enough, wasn't she?

She lay for what seemed like a long time, simply staring into space, not thinking or seeing, but just lying there, and then suddenly she had a vivid memory of how she had felt the night they had danced together, of how precious and desired he had made her feel. Then the tears came, scalding hot and bitter.

She rolled over and reached for the quilt, wrapping herself in it, crying until exhaustion overwhelmed her and she fell into a deep sleep.

IT WAS THE SOUND of the fire that woke her, the cheerful crackle of the logs that reached into her sleep and made her open her eyes sleepily and disbelievingly. But the fire *was* burning, she could see the flames from the bed. The curtains were closed as well, and someone had made the bed properly, putting a pillow under her head and wrapping her tenderly in the quilt.

For some reason she thought it must be her mother, but it wasn't her mother who was standing broodingly beside the fire, his face turned toward the bed, watching her.

She went still, the air whooshing out of her lungs.

'You came back,' she said stupidly.

'I had to. You didn't really think I'd leave you up here on your own, did you?' He came over to the bed and looked down at her. She couldn't help it, she flinched, remembering what she had done, what utter madness had possessed her.

'You've been crying,' he said abruptly. 'Why?'

'Why?' She looked disbelievingly at him. 'Do you really need to ask?' She turned her face away from him and added in a small suffocated voice, 'I

want to apologise... for what... for what I did.
I...I...'

She started to shake violently, and wished she
could close her eyes and simply make him disappear.

'Oh, Sorrel, please don't. I'm the one who ought
to apologise.'

Suddenly he was on the bed beside her, lifting her
in her cocoon of bedding and holding her, rocking
her as though she was an infinitely precious child.

'I'm sorry you've lost him. I'm sorry I hurt you.
I never thought you loved him. I was so sure I could
make you love me, you see—so arrogantly determined that I would make you a better lover, a better husband, that I could teach you to forget your
fear of giving yourself. I was so caught up in my
own desires, that I wouldn't let myself believe that
what you felt for him mattered. What can I say?'

Sorrel had gone still as she listened to him. Was
she really hearing this, or had she started hallucinating? She raised her head from his shoulder and
looked round the room, frowning slightly. Perhaps
this *was* all a dream, wish-fulfilment, a chimera she
had created out of her own need.

'Sorrel...'

It *was* a dream, she decided firmly, and since it
was... She looked up at him and smiled at him, all
her love for him shining in her eyes.

'You don't have to say anything,' she whispered softly. 'All you have to do is show me, Val.'

She heard him gasp, his eyes going black with emotion, and a tiny ripple of concern touched her spine. Was she really capable of dreaming such an intensity of emotion? She decided that she was and nestled against him, giving a faint sigh of anticipation. If she couldn't have Val himself, then she supposed this dream might well be the next best thing.

'Are you saying what I think you're saying?' he asked her uncertainly.

'I don't know,' she answered him promptly. 'Tell me what you think I'm saying, and then I'll let you know.'

'I think you're saying that you want me to do this,' he told her thickly, bending his head to capture her mouth, kissing her with all the fierce sweetness she remembered, so that her bones melted and her body turned fluid in his arms, leaving her with just enough strength to lift her arms and fasten them round his neck as he groaned against her quiescent lips, drinking from the sweetness of her mouth as she gave herself up to him without stint.

This was a very satisfying dream, Sorrel decided happily, clinging to his shoulders, letting her instincts guide her as she closed her mouth round his tongue, caressing it as he had been caressing hers.

The reaction she got made her murmur blissfully deep in her throat, and press herself tightly against him. The quilt was in the way and she pushed crossly at it, murmuring little breathy words of pleasure in his ear as she fumbled with the buttons on his shirt.

He was trembling, actually trembling in her arms. She gave a tiny catlike smile, her eyes slitting with feminine pleasure, her nails flexing against his skin as she tested its satin-hard texture.

A sound not unlike a purr trembled in her throat as she placed her mouth against his skin, tasting its heat. It felt good to touch him like this, to have the strength of him in her arms and to know she had the power to make him tremble like a child.

She heard him speaking to her, the words mumbled and indistinct, felt the cold shaft of air as he pushed her away—and for a moment she thought she was going to lose the dream, but almost immediately he came back to her, and her eyes widened as the firelight enhanced the golden nakedness of his skin.

She let him lift her out of the nest of her quilt, her breasts needing no enticement to reveal her pleasure as he held and caressed them, first with his hands and then with his mouth, her body arching and twisting as fire darts of pleasure she had never imagined tormented it. He was kissing her as she had kissed him: fierce, open-mouthed kisses against her skin, as though he wanted to bite into her and devour her. She made soft murmurs of encouragement, stroking him, teasing him, watching him with passion, heavy eyes, her body voluptuous with pleasure. Since it was only a dream, there was no need to conceal her love, no need to hide her feelings or the little words of praise and invitation that tumbled from her lips. She was even able to laugh when she saw the shock of excitement that ran through him, jerking his body as taut as a bowstring as she told him how much she wanted him and where.

She touched his eyebrows with her fingertips, kissed them with tender lips, bit gently at his throat and let her body mould itself invitingly to his, welcoming the fierce throb of his alien male flesh.

She wanted to touch him there—to caress him and show him how much she gloried in his maleness, but he wouldn't let her, and that didn't seem to fit into her dream. She was free to dream whatever she wanted. It was, after all, her dream. She murmured something to that effect, and heard him laugh shakily and say something about it being his dream too, but adding a rider that on this particular occasion there wasn't going to be time, and all the while he was talking to her his hands were touching her, shaping her and then finally and blissfully caressing her so that she felt she would melt...dissolve...explode and die of the pleasure of that sensation.

She sighed her thoughts aloud and heard him say fiercely, 'Oh, Sorrel, are you trying to drive me out of my mind?' And then he was moving her, holding her, entering her, and her body was accommodating itself to him, loving the feel of him, gathering itself around him so that each thrust of his flesh drew soft whimpers of delight from her lips, and the rhythm he was teaching her was so pleasurable to respond to that the sharp spasm of pain interrupting it was a mere moment's irritation to be brushed aside and forgotten in the growing swell of delight ripening and gathering inside her, awaiting the magical moment of release, which she knew instinctively he would give her if she simply listened to the message of his body.

When it happened, it was more pleasurable than anything she had imagined. More intense, more...more everything, and she told him so dreamily, watching him as the dream slipped away and she returned to oblivion.

She woke up slowly, a soft smile curling her mouth, her eyes hazy with remembered pleasure. The fire still burned and it was dark outside the window. Something wasn't quite right. She frowned and tried to gather her thoughts.

Yes, that was it. The fire should be out, the room cold and empty. After all, that...that mind-destroying pleasure had just been a dream. Val had gone, hours ago.

But he hadn't gone, she realised shakily. He was lying right here beside her, one hard thigh thrust possessively across her body, his breath warming her skin, his arm curling round her, as it had done that first night she had slept here in this bed with him.

She started to tremble violently. 'It wasn't a dream.'

'What wasn't?' Val asked her huskily.

He was awake. It was even worse than she had thought. She swallowed nervously, hardly daring to look at him. When she did, what she saw wasn't reassuring. The quilt they were wrapped in had slipped, revealing his bare chest. There were small dark marks on his flesh from which she hurriedly averted her eyes.

Had she made those telltale small bruises? Had she?

'What wasn't a dream?' he asked her again.

He was leaning up on one elbow now, watching her quietly.

'You...me...this.' She waved her hand in an encompassing gesture, pink colour touching her face. 'I thought...I thought...I thought it was just a dream.'

He had gone very still, and now his free hand cupped her chin, turning her face so that she was forced to look at him.

'Just a dream?' His mouth twisted slightly, and she had the odd feeling that she had hurt him. 'So those very special words you said to me meant nothing, then, Sorrel, is that it?'

'What special words?' she asked him, but she had a sinking feeling that she knew exactly what they were.

'You said you loved me,' he told her inexorably. 'Were you lying?'

Lying... She gave a small soft moan of pain.

'You know I wasn't,' she admitted despairingly, and then she remembered something very important. She stared at him with an arrested expression. There was a look in his eyes that seemed to urge her to leap some final hurdle, to overcome some final obstacle. Her throat went dry, and she dared not look away from him in case she lost her courage; her throat seemed to close up and her voice was a strained plea as she said uncertainly, 'You said *you* loved *me*. Did *you* ... did you mean it?'

'What do you think?' He saw the pain start to dawn in her eyes and said harshly, 'No, Sorrel...listen to your heart, not your mind. Think...remember how it was between us. Do you imagine it could ever have been like that if I didn't?'

She was shaking as much with shock as with relief, unable even now to take it all in; her last rational memory was of him driving away, everything since then had an otherworldly magic about it that had made it seem impossible that any of it had happened.

'Of course I love you,' Val groaned, gathering her into his arms. 'I've loved you from the first moment I saw you. Not that I wanted to admit it. All my life I've had three big sisters bullying me, and now it looked as if they'd won out again.'

Sorrel was completely lost, and a frown puckered her forehead.

'I don't understand.'

Val laughed and hugged her.

'It's simple, really. When I said I was going to look up the Welsh side of the Llewellyn family while I was over here on business, my three bossy sisters warned me that I could end up following in the family tradition and bringing back an English bride.

'I told them they were out of their minds. I was even crazy enough to make a bet on it. I should have known better,' he groaned against her throat. 'I couldn't believe it when I saw you. Couldn't believe it and didn't want to believe it; and then you went and told me you were going to marry another man.'

'I had no idea,' Sorrel said helplessly. 'You never gave any indication.'

'Not to you,' he agreed wryly. 'But the rest of your family weren't slow in putting two and two together. I think your mother's already warned mine to start preparing for a wedding.'

'A wedding?' Sorrel stared at him.

'Of course. You've got to marry me now, you know,' he teased her smugly. 'After all, you've had your wicked way with me. Seduced me...'

'*I* seduced *you*—' Sorrel began indignantly, but he bent his head and placed his lips to her ear, repeating some of the things she had said to him, making her face burn with embarrassed colour and her eyes widen in faint shock.

'I didn't really say that, did I?' she gasped uncertainly.

'That and more...much, much more,' Val assured her.

'I thought it was just a dream.'

'So you kept telling me.'

'Oh, you...you knew I didn't think you were real!' she protested, pushing at his chest. 'And you let me...'

'Let you? I couldn't stop you,' he told her virtuously, and then his eyes danced as he leaned over her and murmured softly, 'I don't suppose you could close your eyes and pretend to have another dream, could you?'

'Another...' Sorrel glared at him indignantly, her face flushed. 'Oh!' She looked at him hesitantly, still not entirely convinced. 'You're not just saying all this because of Andrew...because you feel you've got to marry me...are you?'

He had been laughing, but suddenly he sobered, cupping her face and looking down into her eyes. 'My darling girl, you're right about one thing. I have got to marry you, but not because we've made love, and certainly not because of anything to do with Andrew. I've got to marry you, because quite simply I can't live without you. Perhaps it's something in my genes, I don't know...but when you opened the kitchen door and I saw you standing there, I knew that my life would never be the same again. I knew that I'd met my destiny, following in the footsteps of my ancestor, come to claim the woman he loved.'

A tiny shiver of sensation ran through her, a feeling of something so right that it almost seemed predestined.

'Full circle,' she whispered under her breath. 'Life has turned full circle.' It was a magical, awesome moment charged with an emotion that made her eyes sting with tears as Val took her hand in his, linking their fingers tightly together.

'I can't wait to marry you, Sorrel. To take you home with me.' Suddenly he looked hesitant, almost uncertain, the fierce pleasure dying from his eyes. 'Will you do that, Sorrel? Will you come back to Perth with me as my wife? It will mean leaving this...everything that's familiar to you.'

Sorrel reached up and placed her fingers against his lips.

'Not everything. You'll be there,' she told him quietly, and the way she said it made dark colour burn his skin as he reached for her, muttering her name as he took her in his arms.

'I love you, Sorrel. Lord, how I love you,' he told her, the words muffled against her mouth as she whispered to him that she loved him, too.

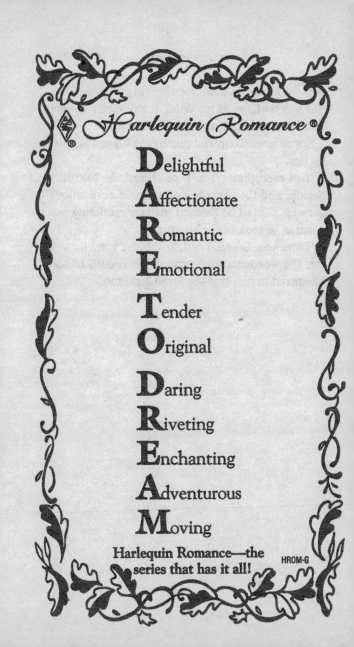

Harlequin Romance ®

Delightful
Affectionate
Romantic
Emotional

Tender
Original

Daring
Riveting
Enchanting
Adventurous
Moving

Harlequin Romance—the
series that has it all!

HROM-G

HARLEQUIN PRESENTS®

HARLEQUIN PRESENTS
men you won't be able to resist falling in love with...

HARLEQUIN PRESENTS
women who have feelings just like your own...

HARLEQUIN PRESENTS
powerful passion in exotic international settings...

HARLEQUIN PRESENTS
intense, dramatic stories that will keep you turning
to the very last page...

HARLEQUIN PRESENTS
The world's bestselling romance series!

Harlequin® Historical

If you're a serious fan of historical romance,
then you're in luck!

Harlequin Historicals brings you
stories by bestselling authors, rising new stars
and talented first-timers.

Ruth Langan & Theresa Michaels
Mary McBride & Cheryl St. John
Margaret Moore & Merline Lovelace
Julie Tetel & Nina Beaumont
Susan Amarillas & Ana Seymour
Deborah Simmons & Linda Castle
Cassandra Austin & Emily French
Miranda Jarrett & Suzanne Barclay
DeLoras Scott & Laurie Grant...

You'll never run out of favorites.

Harlequin Historicals...they're too good to miss!

HARLEQUIN®

I N T R I G U E®

THAT'S INTRIGUE—DYNAMIC ROMANCE AT ITS BEST!

Harlequin Intrigue is now bringing you more—more men and mystery, more desire and danger. If you've been looking for thrilling tales of contemporary passion and sensuous love stories with taut, edge-of-the-seat suspense—then you'll *love* Harlequin Intrigue!

Every month, you'll meet four new heroes who are guaranteed to make your spine tingle and your pulse pound. With them you'll enter into the exciting world of Harlequin Intrigue—where your life is on the line and so is your heart!

Harlequin Intrigue—we'll leave you breathless!

INT-GEN

LOOK FOR OUR FOUR FABULOUS MEN!

Each month some of today's bestselling authors bring
four new fabulous men to Harlequin American Romance.
Whether they're rebel ranchers, millionaire power brokers
or sexy single dads, they're all gallant princes—and
they're all ready to sweep you into lighthearted fantasies
and contemporary fairy tales where anything is possible
and where all your dreams come true!

You don't even have to make a wish...Harlequin American
Romance will grant your every desire!

Look for Harlequin American Romance wherever Harlequin
books are sold!